NATIVES

A NOVEL BY
INONGO-VI-MAKOMÈ

TRANSLATED BY
MICHAEL UGARTE

Phoneme Media
1551 Colorado Blvd., Suite 201
Los Angeles, California 90041

First Edition, 2015

Originally published in Spanish as *Nativas*
by Clavell Cultura SL in 2008.

ISBN: 978-1-939419-45-3

Library of Congress Control Number: 2015947082

This book is distributed by Publishers Group West

Printed in the United States of America

Phoneme Media is a nonprofit publishing and film
production house, a fiscally sponsored project of Pen
Center USA, dedicated to disseminating and promoting
literature in translation through books and film.

www.phonememedia.org

Curious books for curious people

NATIVES

A NOVEL BY
INONGO-VI-MAKOMÈ

TRANSLATED BY
MICHAEL UGARTE

PHONEME
MEDIA
Los Angeles

CHAPTER 1

NIGHT HAD FALLEN OVER THE city. But in a capital like Barcelona, nightfall hardly changed anything, especially not in an office like Montse's: spacious, tastefully decorated, and well illuminated by artificial lights. She had been there since eight in the morning, and outside of a few consultations with colleagues in the adjoining offices, she had not left the area since her arrival that morning.

She stretched as she sat in her armchair, stood up, and put her hands on her hips. A yawn was growing from inside her body. She opened her mouth wide and covered it quickly before returning her left hand to her hip. She exhaled as she approached the wide picture window. She breathed onto the tips of her fingers and touched the windowpane, leaving a hint of mist on the glass. Admiringly, Montse contemplated the vast cityscape in front of her.

Directly before her was the Olympic Port, with dozens of boats anchored in its waters. Their lights, combined with those shining from the lampposts and illuminated the harbor, their reflections zigzagging over the water. The docks edged the eastern horizon of the harbor. Restaurants and cafés offered a variety of delights. A little further out on the sea she saw other lights outlining the silhouettes of two distant ships. The view was truly marvelous from the window of her modernist building's fifteenth floor. But as she stood there gazing out, taking in the scenery, a slight expression of sadness lined her face. Truth be told, she barely had enough time to enjoy all of it. She spent days, sometimes even entire weeks, never so much as approaching this window to take in the view. Day after day she would return to her office and sit down like an automaton, and when she got up it was only to look for paper or a filed document.

She looked at her wristwatch. "Shit, nine o'clock," she said to herself.

She grabbed her bag, put a few papers in it, and turned off the computer. She did the same with the lights as she left the office. She took the private elevator that went directly to the parking lot. As she pressed a button on the key to her luxury vehicle, a beep sounded and the lights flashed. She got in, started the car, and made her way out of the parking garage. The traffic was heavy, so it took her twenty minutes to get home.

"Good evening, Señorita Torres," greeted her doorman as he opened the elevator.

"Good evening, Joseph," she replied laconically.

The elevator stopped at her floor and she entered her apartment. As she wrapped a robe around herself the doorbell rang. She opened the door.

"You still dressed like that?" asked the woman as she made her way in.

"I'm sorry, Roser, I just got in a minute ago."

"That's what the doorman told me."

When Roser was all the way in, Montse shut the door behind her.

"The time got away from me, I didn't realize how late it was until I looked at the clock."

"You shouldn't work so much. Think more of your needs," Roser commented as she sat down in an armchair.

"Look who's talking! You're not exactly the one to give lessons on this. But I'll follow your advice, even though you don't practice what you preach. The thing is, the help is getting stupider every day. You explain something once or twice, but they do it wrong anyway. I'd fire every one of them!"

"Sure, and you'd end up the boss of a department with no employees. You know, I've never had the urge to do that!"

"If you wait a bit, I'll be ready in a minute. I was about to take a shower," Montse said on her way to the bathroom.

"If you're too tired, we can order out. And later, if you're up for it, we can go for a drink. Tomorrow's Saturday. "

Montse turned around.

"You know, staying at home would be okay with me. But we don't have to order out. I've got enough in the fridge, we can just warm it up... we'll open a bottle of wine and have dinner. As for later, we'll see."

"Alright, so while you're in the shower, I'll warm up what's in the fridge. But even if it gets late we should go out for a stroll and see if we can catch us some dates..."

"Catch some dates? I'd like that! But we're like yesterday's bait... So unless someone starving comes along from the North or South Pole, I doubt we'll find anyone out there for us."

"Hey, pretty girl, speak for yourself, I'm still looking good! Very good!" Roser said with a bit of flair

"Sure, we're good-looking. But what's the use if all the guys in this city are either blind or impotent... or gay. That must be it, because how do you explain that two women like us are starved for sex? We're attractive, sensible, not too old."

Roser got up.

"Yes, two mature women, well-to-do executives, and looking good. What a waste!"

"It's exactly the 'executive' part that scares the fish away. They say men like dumb women, and I believe it."

Roser laughed as she went into the kitchen.

"That's just what that jerk Ricard insinuated the other day."

"Yes! But hammerheads like Ricard are not the only fish in the sea—there are others with a little more smarts..."

Montse finally made her way to the bathroom, and came out forty minutes later. After dinner, as they sipped their coffee, Roser remarked:

"It's getting late, I don't know if I want to go out."

"No problem, maybe tomorrow."

Roser finished her coffee and got up.

"I'd like a glass of cognac, how about you?"

"Yes, me too."

Roser went over to the wet bar and served them liquor. She then went into the kitchen with two glasses. Before sitting back down she handed her friend the glass.

"Truth is," she said, "it would have been great to be in the company of a man this evening."

"Who wouldn't want that?" asked Montse. "It's been ages since we've done that. Our latest conquests were total failures."

"Don't remind me, Montse. The last one ejaculated in my hands just while I was putting on his condom..."

Both laughed out loud.

"I could have killed him!" said Montse. "I swear, it's not because I didn't want to. Imagine. After the whole night at the club, dancing, dying to make love. You go over to a guy's place for sex, and it turns out he's a total nothing."

"There're no more men left," continued Montse, wiping tears of laughter from her face. "Do you remember the one I went after at the Paloma, I think it was about two years ago?"

"The Andalusian who squashed you?"

"You mean the one I should have squashed! The idiot tried to get into me, which is just what I wanted, but what I got was his big, shivering dick coming on my chest, and he just laid there on top of me motionless, like a sack of potatoes."

"So maybe he sold potatoes, who knows!" laughed Roser with gusto.

"I don't know what he sold and it didn't matter. After lying there on top of me for awhile so I couldn't breathe, I pushed him off, calling him all kinds of names. *Sorry, sorry, give me another chance*," Montse laughed. "And me, clueless as I am, I believed it! And his second chance was worse than the first. But this time I didn't even let him come. I shoved him out of the room along with his shoes and clothes. He bumped into the door, because his legs were giving out from under him. There he was, stumbling down the stairs, half undressed because I didn't even let him put his pants on."

"You were lucky a neighbor didn't see him, or a family member," Roser said, laughing hysterically.

"It was very late, almost morning. But I swear I wouldn't have cared if anyone saw him. I didn't want that pig in my house a second longer."

"Poor man!" exclaimed Roser.

"Poor man? Poor us, poor me! You can't go around arousing women when you can't keep it up for more than a minute. He told me he was fifty—you'd think he'd be able to hold one."

"He wasn't bad looking. He looked strong. When you showed up with him, I was envious," Roser admitted.

"All a big show!"

"One day we'll get lucky and find a couple of guys with God-gifted pricks."

"And if not two, then just one with a big one! I'm sure we can find one like that," said Montse.

"Just one guy—what will the other one of us do?"

"I mean one for the two of us," answered Montse.

"Not a bad idea, a ménage à trois. We've never done that..."

"It wouldn't have to be exactly like that."

"What do you mean?"

Montse grabbed the bottle of cognac. After serving her friend and herself, she sat down and said:

"Look, I've been thinking about something for a while." She stopped for a second and looked at her friend. "I didn't tell you anything, but I was thinking about it."

"What's this about?"

Montse took a sip.

"Listen, when men want a whore, they know where to go, right? They all know where the streetwalkers are—a brothel, an agency."

"Women can do that too. There are whorehouses for women, agencies too," Roser said. "But you don't think..."

"No, that's not what I mean. I was thinking of something a bit more... well, practical, if you can call it that. I thought maybe between the two of us we could pay for an immigrant..."

"Pay an immigrant to fuck us both?" Roser was stunned.

"Hey, don't say it that way."

"So how do you want me to say it?"

"We could look for a young immigrant, pay him well, and for that, he'll stay with us for a little while, at your place and mine."

Roser stared at her.

"Tell me you're joking!"

"I'm serious. I thought you'd be interested."

"For the love of God, Montse, how can you think such a monstrous thing would interest me?"

"Because I don't think it's monstrous, it's just a matter of survival. You and I have been friends for a long time. Let's take advantage of our social and economic advantages. You were in a bad marriage, divorced not long after the wedding. I didn't even get that far. We're alone now and every day we get further away from finding a man to marry. But at least we could find one to satisfy us. It's normal. Why is it monstrous to look for a person to satisfy our sexual needs?"

Roser remained silent, thinking how to respond.

"I don't know, Montse, I never would have thought of such a thing. I just don't... maybe it's illegal?"

"You haven't thought about it, but I've done a lot of thinking for the both of us. And it's not illegal, I can guarantee it. I'm an economist and a lawyer, so I know what I'm talking about. Listen, we live in a society that's both simple and complicated, where what seems true is not always so. You know, 'things aren't always what they seem.' Some people take advantage of that. Why can't we?" She was silent for a minute, then she added, "We'll do it."

"But how? Where are we going to find this guy?"

"We'll find him. There are lots of immigrants around. It won't be hard to find one. Besides, it'll be an act of charity."

"An act of charity to rent someone to make love?"

"You said it! You said the right word: love. All acts of charity come from love, it all comes back to both parties: the one who gives and the one who receives. The donor does it for various reasons: personal satisfaction, solidarity with fellow human beings, satisfying your conscience, whatever. The one who receives doesn't know about this. No need. He only thinks he's fortunate. He returns the favor by being humble and giving thanks. The benefactor immediately feels he's been compensated. It's the same for the believer. He performs acts of charity because he loves God, and that's just what God wants. So to fulfill this mission, he hopes God will pay him back by sending him to heaven."

"It's not the same..."

"It's exactly the same. We're looking for a poor man. We solve his problems by giving him money in exchange for the pleasures we need. I don't see a difference."

"I don't know, Montse. I never thought you would think of such a thing. It's sketchy, don't you think?"

"No, not at all. Look, sweetie, if we saw inside the homes of our native city, you'd be speechless about what happens in them. Far worse things than what I'm proposing. We're going to do this because we need to."

They were silent for a few moments, during the lull in which they took a few sips of their cognac.

"How and when do you think we're gong to do this?" Roser asked, doubting the whole idea.

"Well, now that we've talked about it, I think we should get to it right away, without delay. It's the weekend, so we could begin our search tomorrow."

"Tomorrow?" stammered Montse. "Shouldn't we wait a little?"

Montse shook her head.

"The sooner we decide, the sooner we'll know how to prepare for it. If we hesitate, we'll come up with a bunch of excuses."

"I think it's too fast."

Montse shook her head.

"I'm convinced that the sooner we get this going, the better."

"So what should we do?"

Montse did not have to think about her reply:

"Tomorrow is Saturday. At mid-morning I'll go to the Plaza de Cataluña. That's where I'll start looking. If I don't find anything worthwhile tomorrow, I'll go back the day after."

"So what do I do in the meantime?"

"Well, for example, you can go shopping for a jacket or sweater just in case the person I choose needs clothes."

"So I don't suppose you're going for the poorest one?"

Montse laughed.

"We don't know what destiny will bring, we'll just rely on luck. We'd reject the poorest guy for other reasons, but not for being in need, because that is precisely what we are looking for. We want to share with him."

"Please, Montse, let's keep talking, but don't tell me more about charity. You're convincing me, but let's not confuse this with charity—I really doubt..."

"Fine, so I won't mention charity again! But you know very well we live in a culture where charity is everywhere. We invented it and we put it into practice the moment we took control of the world. My entire family, my mother most of all, knows all about charity. But let's keep to our plan."

"You haven't said anything about what kind of immigrant we're looking for."

"I was thinking of a Black man or an Arab. But I don't trust Arabs."

"Blacks have diseases, AIDS and all that," said Roser, grimacing.

"Diseases are no problem. Here in the first world we've created a utopia. We have medicines to remedy diseases. We have contraception that you and I have used when we've been with white men. We've dealt with our problems and we've solved them, so let's take advantage of our achievements."

"But a Black man!"

"Well," Montse mocked, "you went to bed with one in Cuba three years ago, remember? From what I recall, it wasn't too bad."

"He was a mulatto."

"A white father and a Black mother, or the other way around."

"Yes! But..."

"I'm thirsty, how about we open the bottle of champagne I've got in the fridge?"

"I like that idea. But use the local word, Cava. Maybe with Cava, ideas will come to us."

"Okay, I'll say Cava and not champagne! But it's a good idea, you'll see. If Cava brings us ideas and spirits, all the better."

Montse grabbed the bottle of Cava and poured two glasses. Roser was about to drink when Montse interrupted her:

"Let's toast to the success of our endeavor."

"You mean our craziness."

"Not at all. To the future success of everything we're planning," she touched her glass to Roser's.

"To all that and to whatever God wishes," Roser echoed the toast.

They drank.

"Well, how do you propose to nab a Black guy in this city?" asked Roser. "Lots of people know us. Where are we going to take him? Most of your family members live in this building. They own it! How are you going to take a Black lover into your apartment?"

"I've thought of all that," Montse replied. "My biggest concern is my two gossipy aunts who live upstairs. The rest are no problem. My parents live outside the city, and they never come by without telling me. As far as the doorman is concerned, I'll just use the parking lot elevator. But if everything goes well, after awhile I'll just tell him our man is working on my apartment. I don't think that'll surprise anyone. The aunts upstairs boast about the Black foreman who worked on their parents' plantation in Cuba."

"Do you think there was any hanky-panky?"

"What?"

"The Black foreman and your aunts."

"I don't think so. They were too young, and then they came back crying about Fidel's revolution, and before that, the disaster with the US. But my great-grandfather prepared for all that—he had already started moving his money to Spain," explained

Montse. "But it wouldn't have been bad if there had been some hanky-panky. Actually, a good-sized cock would have made them less chatty. And that's just what I'm looking for, a good prick so I don't turn into a gossipy old hag like them."

The alcohol vapors were beginning to go to their heads.

"I see that you've thought all this out, and that's good."

"Sure thing. Tomorrow we'll do it and we'll do it well. I don't believe in luck. We will make it happen."

"Let's toast to success!" Roser took a good swig.

Montse lifted her glass and drank.

"Yes, let's hear it for success. Tomorrow you'll have it, and you'll have the first turn."

"Me first?"

"Yes, you! If the hunt is successful, I'll bring the prey to your house. We'll take a look at him together, and then he'll stay the night with you. Sunday I'll come by to pick him up, and Monday he'll go back to you."

"So I'll be the guinea pig. Well, I accept."

"That's what I like to hear, girl. And if we agree it's working out, he'll be with you one week and with me the next."

When they finished the bottle of Cava it was five in the morning. They went to bed dizzy. Roser slept in the guest room next to Montse's.

CHAPTER 2

IN THE MORNING AROUND TEN, Montse got out of bed and woke up Roser. After breakfast Montse was ready to begin her project.

"Now, let's get to work!"

Roser looked puzzled.

"Are you sure what we talked about yesterday wasn't just a joke?"

"I've never been more serious! Go get a nice sports jacket or something a guy would wear, then we'll see."

"I thought it was all a bad dream."

"Not at all, it was a good dream, and I'm sure it'll come true."

They both went out onto the street. Montse had put on a pair of jeans and a matching shirt. Over the shirt she wore a large wool jacket. She liked to wear loose-fitting clothes to hide her enormous bulk.

They parted ways as Roser went to her own place to change. When Montse arrived at the Plaza de Cataluña, it was around noon, according to a clock on the upper part of a bank building. She looked at it instinctively.

The plaza was crowded. Children and a few tourists were playing with the pigeons. A mid-autumn sun shone brilliantly. This was perfect for Montse. She put on her sunglasses, took out a hat from her purse and put it on. Then, like any tourist, she started walking around the plaza, observing the wooden park benches where she thought she might find an immigrant. She had seen a couple of men who looked Arab, so she approached them. They looked like good possibilities, but she decided to keep looking. A little further on she saw three Black men and an Arab.

"Too many in one place," she said to herself.

She went over to one of the street vendors and bought a pack of pigeon feed. She looked for a place to sit. Close to the corner of the plaza contiguous to the big department stores there was an entire bench with no one sitting on it. She opened the bag of pigeon feed and began throwing some of the kernels to the birds, so that they would follow her as she strolled over to the bench. As she got to the bench a flock of pigeons fluttered close to her, pecking at the feed she had dropped for them.

When she sat down, she threw out another fistful as far from her as she could. Nonetheless a few of them landed close to her; several pigeons approached her feet. She was amused by their persistence. She contemplated how pleasant these moments could be when she had the time to enjoy them, a little solitary diversion in the middle of the crowded city. She could not remember when she had enjoyed herself more. To think that this plaza and these birds were in Barcelona, just like her... She remembered her parents had brought her here as a child, to play with her friends in this very plaza. But she had never come back. What a shame!

She looked around intently. A few trees that had not yet shed their leaves cast a shadow over the part of the bench where she was sitting. On the branches, birds were chirping, hidden from Montse's sight. She tried to catch a glimpse of them as she shifted her head and removed her sunglasses. As she observed the branches of those nearby trees, she thought of spring. It was the season she loved the best. It changed her mood automatically. It made her happy. She told herself she would return to this spot next spring to see the trees in all their shiny brilliance.

A clock in the neighborhood chimed one in the afternoon. It was then that a young Black man sat down at the other end of the shaded bench. He did this timidly so as not to bother the woman next to him.

Montse looked at him discreetly. She could not see his face clearly because the shadow of a tree was covering part of it. But her heart began to beat a bit faster than normal. It was one thing to conjure up her plan and another to put it into practice.

The young man set aside a bag he was carrying. Montse removed her sunglasses in order to see him better. At that moment he looked away from her. Montse was surprised; she had no recourse but to say hello with her hand. The young man replied in kind and opened his mouth. Despite the distance, the native woman could see his brilliantly white teeth.

Montse doubted if she should strike up a conversation right away or if she should wait for another opportunity. As she pondered, she noticed the young immigrant was averting her gaze. Over on the opposite side of the plaza a group of Latin American musicians had just begun playing tunes with their indigenous instruments. She also looked in that direction. As she contemplated the assembled crowd, she felt something touch her feet. It was a ball. A little further away a child was running toward her in pursuit of the ball as his father followed behind. Montse put her sunglasses and hat back on as the ball rolled under the bench toward the spot where the Black man was sitting.

The boy passed by Montse, looking to recover his ball. When he saw the Black man he stopped and looked at him. The boy was about four years old. The African man looked at him tenderly.

"Hola," he said.

The boy looked around for his father, who had just arrived where Montse was sitting. She had crossed her legs and was looking at the musicians, although from the corner of her eye she did not ignore what was going on at the other side of the bench.

When the boy's father arrived, the Black man had already picked up the ball and offered it to the little one.

"Hola," he said again affably.

The boy clung to his father and looked up at his face.

"Say hello to the gentleman, Jordi," he said as he looked back at his son.

The boy first looked down, but then he stared at the Black man without answering his greeting. He grabbed the ball with his two hands and turned and hid between the legs of his father.

The father said to his son in Catalan, "Say thank you to the gentleman, Jordi."

The boy turned around and ran off toward the center of the plaza. His father followed, but before he left he turned to the immigrant and said, "Gracias."

Both left the scene, and Latin American music resonated through the rest of the plaza. More and more people were slowly arriving. Some youngsters who looked Central European had taken off their shirts as they sat in the grass, sunbathing near the fountain.

Montse removed her glasses and looked at the African. She was determined to approach him and strike up a conversation. The African was looking the other way.

"Hola," greeted Montse in a tone a bit louder than before.

The immigrant looked at her.

"Hola," the native said again, making sure he knew she was talking to him.

"Hello," replied the African clearly as soon as he realized she was addressing him.

"Where are you from?" she asked.

"Africa." He immediately added, "Mali."

Like most Black Africans he identified himself as being from the continent first and then added his country of origin. The degrading economic conditions that had converted that mythical land into a continent of beggars means that their nationality is an afterthought.

"Ah, have you been here for a long time?"

The immigrant could not hear Montse well, so he moved about half a yard closer to her.

"So, have you been here for a long time?" she asked again.

"Oh, yes. Not much... not long... a year..."

"That's nice," she said.

"You from here?" The African had noticed a certain friendliness on the face of the native. This gave him confidence. He had come across friendly people before who asked him that kind of question.

"Yes, I'm from here, from Barcelona."

The immigrant nodded. The native wanted to get right to the point in order to settle the issue that had brought her there, but at the same time she knew she had to be discreet. After all, they were in a public place. She was concerned that anyone she knew could pass by and figure out what was going on. But that wouldn't be too large a problem. Many people frequented Plaza de Cataluña. So when she said, "I like to come here to sit and observe people," she had already justified why she was there. Her new acquaintance, in turn, would probably figure out that this was a custom unknown to him.

But the problem remained: How was she going to bring up what had led her there? She had taken a good look at him. He was probably about twenty-eight. But then again who can guess how old Black people are? He was quite handsome. He was dressed in jeans and a shirt without a logo or print. She was surprised he was not wearing a sweater or a jacket.

"Aren't you cold?"

"No, I not cold," explained the Black man, showing his white teeth.

"Do you live close by?"

The African thought about the question. He gestured with his hands.

"I no have big house."

What he meant to say was that he did not have a permanent house. Actually he did not have any place to stay. That plaza had been his residence for a long time, and any one of those benches had served as his bed, including last night. But Montse did not understand the meaning of "big house."

The native woman looked around to make sure no one was listening to their conversation.

"Why did you come to Spain?"

The African moved and gestured with his head.

"I come look for life. Africa now not good place for make life. No work for young people, lots of poor."

The immigrant realized that using those words touched the natives' nerves. This had worked on other occasions. He had come across men and women who had given him a couple of coins after a conversation like this. He knew that in the culture of charity that prevailed in the West, the needy had to use those kinds of words to achieve their ends.

"Are you working now?"

"Me? Oh, I no have work, I look for..."

This was enough for Montse to conclude that this man was perfect for what she had in mind. As soon as he was cleaned up, he would be more acceptable. He was young, but at the same time he was not young enough to be her grandson. She was forty-eight, and Roser forty-nine. They were twice his age, but what did it matter? They were looking for a man, not an old-timer. On the other hand, looking for a man in a public place like the Plaza de Cataluña was not the least bit comfortable. It was not easy, much less considering that this guy was an immigrant and, on top of that, Black.

Montse had made her decision: If he accepted, they would try this guy out.

"What's your name?"

"Bambara Keita."

"Bambara Keita. Pretty name."

"Yes. And you?"

"Montse."

"Montse. Very nice."

"Do you want to work, Bambara Keita?"

That question surprised the immigrant. From the moment he set foot on the plaza no one had offered him a job. He looked at the woman. She was smiling. He didn't think it was possible. He had heard so many stories. But despite his youth, he was savvy; he had had some adventures. Many of them. Crossing the barriers that separate Melilla from Morocco was not easy. The Spanish border guards had beaten him when they'd caught him, and put him in jail with others like him. Then there was the little detention camp where they warehoused them—the place they euphemistically called the "Reception Camp"—to say nothing of his ordeal crossing the desert. He did not want to think about all that. He had arrived, and it was heaven. Every day he thanked God for his perilous journey and successful arrival. Indeed God could be the one who had sent this woman his way to offer help on this afternoon.

"Yes, want work, anytime, any place."

Montse smiled at him again.

"Fine. If you want to work, you have to come with me. A friend of mine and I will give you work."

"Come now?"

"Yes, now! I mean, if you're interested, because I have to go now."

The immigrant stood up and picked up the bag with his belongings.

"Let's go," said Montse.

Montse was ready to leave. She had to cross a street flanked by big department stores and go down to the parking garage to pick up her car. The African was at her side, but Montse did all she could to pretend they were not together. The affluence of the passersby helped. The immigrant understood that the native did not want people to think that they had any relation. He remained silent and kept a guarded distance.

They went down to the parking garage, where she unlocked the door to her car with the remote, started the vehicle, and took off. As soon as she left the garage, she grabbed her cell phone and called Roser.

"We're on our way."

"On your way? You mean you've found someone?" asked Roser.

"Yes, and we'll be at your place in about fifteen minutes. Or less."

Montse did not wait for a response. She hung up and floored the accelerator.

CHAPTER 3

WHEN ROSER OPENED THE DOOR for them, Montse was relieved.

"Roser, this is Bambara Keita," she announced as Roser shut the door.

Roser turned to the man and offered her hand.

"Pleased to meet you, Ba... ba..."

"Bambara Keita. Bam-ba-ra Kei-ta," Montse repeated.

"Bam-ba-ra Kei-ta," Roser mimicked, trying to pronounce each syllable.

The African extended his hand as he nodded vigorously up and down, giving his approval of the pronunciation of his name.

"A little difficult, don't you think?" she was addressing Montse.

"Something like Villacampa Bosch, but in African," said Montse.

Then she turned to Bambara Keita:

"Sit down, Bambara Keita. This house is yours, don't be afraid of anything. You can leave your bag right there."

She followed her words with a hand signal. The immigrant put his bag on the floor and sat down. He did not do so abruptly. He was a bit scared. His body had never rested in such a luxurious chair.

Roser noticed his hesitation.

"Please sit down. Make yourself at home."

Bambara Keita sat down. The cushion gave way a little. He thought for a moment that he would fall back. But he maintained his balance even though he was not at ease.

The two women observed this stranger from another land carefully, as they associated his uncertainty with the control they had over him.

"Would you like a drink or something?" asked Montse, the first to respond.

The African was still intimidated by the situation and could only shrug his shoulders.

"I'll bring you something to drink," said Montse. "Let's step into the kitchen for a minute, Roser."

Roser automatically did what she was told.

"What do you think?" Montse was anxious to know as soon as they entered the kitchen.

"He's a child," she stammered.

"But not a baby. Maybe he can be our child," Montse affirmed.

Roser was silent for a moment. She was disarmed by the rapidity of her friend's responses.

"He's a little dirty and smells a bit, don't you think?" she said, trying to react.

"That's why I told you to buy him some clothes. Now we'll tell him to take a shower, change his clothes, eat something—just like we said—and then we'll tell him what we expect from him," explained Montse confidently.

As the two women planned their next move in the kitchen, Bambara Keita waited in the dining room. His mind was blank. He looked from one side of the room to the other. It was a large space, tastefully decorated with a round glass table and four chairs surrounding it, a leather upholstered sofa with matching chairs (including the one he was sitting on), a couple of arm chairs, a round coffee table between the sofa and chairs, several portraits on the walls, lamps, and other fine furnishings. No, Bambara Keita did not know how to describe the style or the quality of the items that adorned the dwelling and made it look so beautiful. It all belonged to these two women who had not yet told them what they wanted of him.

The two natives appeared. Montse was holding a glass of juice. She offered it to him.

"Thank you," said the guest.

Montse sat down next to him, and Roser sat at their side in one of the armchairs.

Bambara Keita drank his juice. He did not know if it was proper to drink it in one gulp or in sips. Montse's words settled his indecision momentarily.

"As I told you, my friend and I are going to give you work. There is no hurry. You can take a shower. I think we have some clean clothes you can wear. Then we'll eat, and then we'll tell you about your work."

As Montse spoke, the immigrant was finishing his drink, but there was another problem: he didn't know where to put the glass—on the floor? The rug? The table?

Roser—who was looking at the Black man with, at once, disdain and something else she could not identify—extended her hand and grabbed the glass. She placed it on the table next to her visitor.

"You can leave the glass here."

The African thanked her for her graciousness. He had already learned something new in that house.

"Are you okay with that, Bambara Keita?" asked Montse with a big smile on her face.

"Oh, yes!" he replied quickly.

He was not certain exactly what his benefactor had proposed, but he accepted.

"Well, get up and come along over here. Roser will show you the bathroom."

Roser got up and led him to the washroom, which had a small shower stall.

"Here is the shampoo and body lotion. This is the faucet for hot water, and this one for cold. There is a towel over here, and here are your clothes."

It was then that Bambara Keita understood what Montse was proposing. He did not react for a moment. He did not know what to do or what to say. Everything was moving too fast.

"Everything okay?" asked Roser, forcing a smile.

The African reacted. "Oh, yes, but must get—"

He went back to the dining room and grabbed his bag. This move made the two women uneasy. It all went so fast that Montse was at a loss for words. She stammered, "Aren't you happy?"

"Oh, yes, me happy, but want something in bag."

The two women understood. Bambara Keita entered the bathroom. They listened for the door to close from the inside.

"For a moment I thought he was about to leave." Roser seemed a little disappointed.

"I was a little worried too."

"Aren't we taking this joke a bit too far, Montse?"

"It's not a joke, Roser. It's an adventure. Doesn't it excite you? It does me, more every day."

"So..." Roser could not finish what she was going to say.

"So? What? Just say it! There's still time to tweak the plan."

"Montse, tell me we're not doing anything illegal or immoral."

Montse approached her and took her by the shoulders.

"I don't have to tell you anything, Roser. You know it. We're not doing anything illegal or immoral. It would be illegal if we killed him. Are we going to kill him?"

"No!" Roser replied immediately.

"Well then take it easy. We're not doing anything wrong. We're just going to satisfy the basic human needs of any human being, any child of Mother Nature. The urge for sexual pleasure is natural, the same as eating when you're hungry, drinking when you're thirsty, or relieving yourself when your body asks for it. How many times have you kept yourself from drinking water when you were thirsty?"

Roser did not answer.

"Well, there you go," said Montse triumphantly. "It's the same as making love. We deprive ourselves of it. We keep our bodies from the pleasure of having all our necessities satisfied. I mean our bodily needs. If you tell me right now that you don't suffer from sexual hunger in this gigantic city of ours, I'll believe you, and when that kid comes out I'll tell him to leave."

Roser did not know what to say.

"I know what you're saying, Montse, it's just that—"

"It's just nothing, Roser! We're going to live our adventure, if it doesn't come out all right, so what? At least we'll know we tried. That's the life of humans on this earth. Some people, through religion, or ethics, or whatever, have tried to change it, modify it, but they have not been able to. What you and I are trying to do is not new. Others do it, surely more than you or I can imagine. The problem is that hypocrisy, which is part of our culture, camouflages it, or at least it tries to. But it's all over the place. It's in our world, our culture." She embraced her friend. "It'll turn out fine, let's hope for the best."

Roser hugged her back.

Back in the bathroom, Bambara Keita had taken off his clothes. He did not want to think too much about anything. He thought he might have been dreaming. But it didn't matter. Either in dreams or in real life, certain events have great effect on us.

He was enjoying a sweet, agreeable moment. If it were a dream, he would wake up and continue with his everyday life. And if he was not dreaming, all the better.

That morning, like all mornings, he had prayed to God when he rose from his makeshift cot. He stayed at the entrance to a bank near the plaza where he met the woman. He gave thanks to God for having gotten to this point in his life, and then he asked Him for a little luck to get out of it.

He could not tell for sure if what had happened that day was an answer to his morning prayer. Whatever it was, he had a shower within reach and he was going to take advantage of it. He remembered what his grandfather told him: people should always go about life clean, because no one ever knows when it is his time to die. If you die clean, you will enter the realm of the ancestors.

The Pentecostal preachers convinced him with time to replace the realm of the ancestors with God's paradise, but he always lived up to his grandfather's lesson about the importance of cleanliness. If death catches you by surprise, at least you'll be clean when you go to heaven with God.

He didn't know what these two women wanted from him, but he was going to take a shower. If they wanted him dead, at least he'd be clean in heaven. Thinking all that, he took a little plastic bag from the bigger bag. That was where he kept an old razor. He shaved. Then he put the razor back and took out a washcloth.

He went into the shower stall. He followed Roser's instructions and turned on the hot water, trying to regulate the temperature with cold water. He let the water cascade over his body, and he was thankful. He did not remember exactly how long it had been since his last shower. He had taken advantage of a few public showers, but in Barcelona they were a luxury and there was not enough of them. He realized he hadn't been able to shower in about three weeks.

He turned the faucet on all the way. The drops of water stung his skin, but he didn't care about the pain.

Without shutting off the faucet he applied the body gel. He then scrubbed his entire body with the washcloth. When he saw the dark water flow into the drain, he thought for a moment that he had spilled a jar of black paint, but immediately figured out that it was his own dirt. All that thick, dark foam flowed away with the water. Again he lathered from head to toe, rubbing his body with the washcloth and then rinsing. He performed this operation several times, making sure the water that flowed over his body was no longer dark but white with soap.

When he finished and shut off the faucet, he realized what a disaster he had caused. The small bathroom was flooded.

"My god!" he exclaimed in his mother tongue.

He looked at the floor several times without knowing what to do. When he entered the shower stall he had noticed some glass doors, but he had never seen anything like that except in movies. He had tried to figure out how the doors opened and closed, but he couldn't.

"Now what?"

He didn't think twice. He grabbed his shirt and pants and turned them into a mop. Then, just like that, he leaned over and started to dry the floor.

When the floor was minimally dry, he put his wet clothes in his bag. He dried himself with a towel, and then he took out a jar of body cream and applied it to his whole body. Without cream, Black skin whitens and looks dirty. He wanted to avoid that.

"Montse, what the devil is that kid doing in the bathroom?"

The two were standing around the dining room table after arranging it for dinner.

"He'll be right in," Montse reassured her.

"He'll be right in! When? He's been in there for over an hour. Has something happened to him?"

"Don't worry. He's alive, I've gone over to the bathroom door a few times. I heard something."

They kept waiting.

CHAPTER 4

MONTSE AND ROSER WERE SITTING in their lounge chairs in the living room. They heard something coming from that part of the flat. They both looked down the hallway leading to the bathroom and saw the door open. When they saw him they were speechless.

Bambara Keita was wearing the red jacket that Roser had bought that morning. She had chosen it as if she knew the person who was going to wear it. The blackness of his face shone brilliantly, magnificently. The ashen tone from the city's dirt had disappeared. His six-foot stature dominated the room.

Montse was taken by surprise.

"Bambara Keita, you look so handsome!"

She bounded off her chair and approached him. She grabbed his hand and led him to Roser.

"Isn't he beautiful, Roser?"

"Yes, he really is!"

Montse ran her fingers through his hair.

"Your hair is moist," she said sweetly.

Bambara Keita didn't know quite what to do or say. He was still holding his bag.

"Give me your bag. We can keep it in the utility room."

Roser did not wait for the African's response. She took it from him and brought it to one of the utility closets. Meanwhile Montse kept staring at him. The Black man didn't know what to do with himself, where to go, and much less how to respond to so much praise. Fortunately for him, Blacks don't blush. At least that's what people think.

"Come sit down over here. We're going to have something to eat."

Montse sat the immigrant down in front of his plate. Then she went into the kitchen. Roser followed.

"Tell me, Montse, do Black people get tanned?"

"What are you saying!"

"It's just that it looks like parts of the shower stall have shoe polish stains."

"It's probably because he was really dirty. Poor guy."

"Poor guy? You mean my poor shower and those poor little fish in the Besós River, and those poor fish in the sea!" Roser said with feigned pity.

"Don't worry about the river, it's been a while since there were any fish there. And if a couple of fish in the sea die, what does it matter? We are about to live again. And I don't know why you're complaining about your bathroom. On Monday your cleaning lady will come by and leave it sparkling."

"No way. I'm not leaving the bathroom like that until Monday. What am I going to tell the cleaning lady? She'll think I let a gorilla in my bathroom."

"Ay, Roser, please don't say that. You're paying your housekeeper to clean, not to ask questions. Anyway, I'll clean it later, if you wish," she said, trying to change the subject. "Isn't he cute? Hasn't this been worth it?"

"Well, I admit he's not bad for a Black man... Yes, not bad."

"What do you mean, not bad? He's beautiful!"

They brought the dishes to the table. Roser sat to the right of Bambara Keita and Montse to the left. In the middle of the table there was a salad and a steaming paella. Roser, the host, served the invited guest first.

"Go ahead and eat," she said to him.

Bambara Keita nodded and smiled showing his teeth, but he did nothing else. Before proceeding he observed what his companions did. He had copied their movements, starting with placing the napkin over his lap. He couldn't begin eating without seeing their movements.

In the meantime, Montse poured wine into the glasses in front of each plate.

"I didn't ask you if you drink alcohol," said Montse.

"Oh, yes, no problem."

"I know there are many Muslims in Mali."

"Yes, Christians too. I Christian."

"Ah, all the better. Right, Roser?"

"Sure," the other one said without paying much attention.

When she finished serving, Roser said, "Let's eat. I hope you like my paella."

Bambara Keita observed how the women held their forks as they dipped into that golden rice. Damn, he had always eaten it with a spoon! He held the fork, dipped it into the rice, and brought it to his mouth. It was very good. He asked himself why white people were so particular at times. The paella would have been so much better if he could eat it with a spoon.

Roser, disdainfully observing her guest's movements, noticed that he was not at ease.

"You can eat the paella with a spoon. Many people eat it that way."

That comment also made Montse aware of the African's differences.

"In my mom's hometown they eat it that way."

She accompanied her new friend in his wish. She began eating the paella with a spoon. Bambara Keita was encouraged by this. He switched from the fork to the spoon, and the paella tasted much better to him.

"We haven't toasted. Let' do it!" Montse lifted her glass.

The others followed.

"To our getting together. To everything. May our endeavor be successful!"

They chimed their glasses then drank. Bambara Keita gulped, coughed, and almost lost everything he had eaten to that point. The women watched as he turned his back to them. Montse poured some water and gave it to him.

"Drink, this will help it pass."

The African drank.

"The boy doesn't seem accustomed to fine wines," said Roser, not without a hint of sarcasm.

Montse gave her a little kick under the table with her foot.

"You OKAY?"

"Yes," answered the African with a hoarse voice.

His eyes were red; tears were streaming down his face.

"Don't you like this wine?" asked Montse, trying to relieve his discomfort.

"Oh, yes, wine good, but what happened?" Then he smiled. "The rice good, I eat too fast?" His naivete regarding the habits of his hosts would redeem him, he thought.

They all laughed.

"That's right. Roser's paella is delicious. Mine's good too, some day you'll see."

They continued eating. Bambara Keita had learned another lesson and had taken measures as a result. He was now sipping the wine. He had never tried a wine like the kind his hosts were offering him. His palate was accustomed to the type sold in boxes, common in the bars and stores. Pure poison, some people claimed. But they said this just after drinking a bit too much of the "poison." Bambara Keita was accustomed to the taste of that bad wine. On this table there was an aged Rioja he had never had before, and it tasted a bit strange, like medicine. He wondered why his hosts had such bad taste. Where in hell had they found such a horrible wine? He realized the boxed wine was bad, but at least it reminded him of home. The Spanish Rioja was a little better quality, but it was not at all like the mixture of vinegar and quinine he was used to. But if that's what civilized people like his new rich friends were drinking, he would do so as well. This is why he had risked his life to get to Europe. He had come to find life! To enjoy the flavors and pleasures of civilization.

As he ate, he noticed that Montse placed her hand on his when she wanted to tell him something. But he still had not figured out what kind of work those two angels were about to offer him.

After the main dishes, there were desserts, then coffee, but he turned them down.

"Don't you even want tea? We have regular and chamomile."

Bambara Keita did not know what chamomile was. He had had tea before, and he would have liked some, but he told himself he had had enough that day.

When the two women had cleared the table they talked in the kitchen, out of the African's listening range. Finally they went back to the dining room. Roser, a constant smoker, always had a cigarette between her fingers. As she plunged into one of the armchairs, Montse did the same next to Bambara Keita. She nuzzled close to him and placed her hand on his lap.

"Well, Bambara Keita, you say you want to work and we want to offer it to you." Montse paused to listen to his response.

"Yes, want work. I came for work."

"Well then. You're going to work with both of us, but it won't be anything like you might think. It will be simple. Roser and I will pay you a thousand euros a month. Each of us will give you five hundred. You'll be able to find an apartment, or a nice room."

Bambara Keita could not believe his good luck. It was true that he had prayed intensely that morning, perhaps even with a tone of urgency, but never without humility: *Lord, how can I live like an animal in the midst of such abundance and richness? You, oh Lord, you who have made it possible for me to arrive to this land of whites, why are you abandoning me? Nevertheless, Lord, I am your faithful servant, and I know you have a place for all of your servants. I will do what you wish. Whatever sign you send me, I will know what to do.*

"What do you think?"

Montse asked this question as she caressed him softly, his face this time. He was a bit distracted by the memory of his conversation with God that morning, knelt down in the bank entrance with a couple of white homeless people.

"Oh, yes. Very good, thank you," he said to break the silence.

"So a thousand euros is all right with you?"

A thousand euros! God! A thousand euros! Was he dreaming? Is this the way life works? So many years of suffering and misery, and here was someone talking about a thousand euros. No more, no less than a thousand euros! His head calculated the amount in African francs. That's six hundred thousand and five African francs! A fortune. A sum that not even doctors earned, nor even those who had studied the white man's science.

"But if that's not enough for you, we can make adjustments."

Roser coughed. Bambara Keita noticed the cough and came back to reality.

"Oh, yes, all good, very good!"

Montse slipped her hand further down between the African's legs.

"But you have not asked what kind of work you have to do for us."

"I do everything. I want work, all work." The African quickly responded by declaring his wishes.

Roser remained silent, looking at both of them without noticing the details of the conversation or her friend's gestures.

"Before we explain what we want of you, tell us how old you are."

"My years?"

"Yes, how-ma-ny-years-you-have."

"Oh, yes. I thirty-three."

"Thirty-three?" Montse was surprised.

"Yes."

Suddenly the African's face flushed with worry. Would his age be an obstacle to acquiring the job? His heartbeat quickened.

"How do you look so young?" It was the first time Roser had contributed to the conversation.

"You don't look that age. I thought you were about twenty-seven."

Bambara Keita began to think that a few years too many might be a problem. So he added, "But I do all work. Strong."

"We don't doubt it, Bambara Keita. That age is fine for what we want from you." Montse set his mind at ease. "You are the same age as Christ."

"And we are Mary's age. His mother," Roser added sarcastically.

"Don't blaspheme." Montse laughed.

"I was only finishing your thought."

"Well, Bambara Keita, the work we have for you is simple. It has to do with being with each one of us."

Roser could not stand it any more; her nerves were shot. She got up.

"I'm going to get a glass of water."

She started for the kitchen, but she didn't make it. She stood in a corner and without their noticing she listened to what the other two were saying.

"Have you heard what I've told you, Bambara Keita?"

"Yes, I with you. Okay, yes."

But Montse was still not convinced the immigrant understood exactly what services were expected of him in exchange for the thousand euros a month.

"You be with us, no... You have to *be* with us. I'm saying that you make love with me and with Roser."

Roser, standing in her little hiding place, forced her eyes shut. She wanted the earth to open up beneath her.

"Oh, good, you good. I like."

Once the puzzle was solved, Montse relaxed. She followed her words with more caresses.

"You're going to have two women just for you. Can you handle that?"

Bambara Keita also regained confidence. His previous worries had disappeared as if by magic.

"Oh, yes, I can with you two. My father says a fish does not make a bird."

"And what does that mean?" asked Montse tenderly.

"Because now I know I my father's son. He: three wives. I now two."

Montse almost choked. She saw Roser clench her fists. She got up and approached her.

"Okay, Roser. I'm going to get something from the kitchen— come along." She led her into the kitchen.

"I can't stand this Black guy any more. I'm going to kick him out right now."

"But what did he do?" Montse asked, trying to lessen her friend's anxieties.

"What has he done? You think that stupid remark is okay?"

"He just repeated a saying from his town. An interesting saying, actually. A fish does not give birth to a bird. That's wise!"

"For you it's wise, for me it's—it's— Comparing us to his father's wives. What a joke!"

"Alright, look at it another way. A man that sleeps with two women, you can say they are his wives. The same as a woman who does it with two men, she could say that both are her husbands.

Maybe we're just used to the word lover instead of husband or wife."

"I don't know. This is driving me crazy."

"I thought you were beginning to like him. He's very handsome. Let's keep the plan going. Let's not ruin it now that we've come so far."

Roser was calmer now. They went back to the living room where Bambara Keita was waiting. The two women sat down where they were sitting before. Now more sure of herself, Montse put her hand on the immigrant's leg.

Bambara Keita took advantage of the moment to carefully observe the two women. Until then he had not had time to look them in the face since he had been in their apartment. He felt hampered by the tradition of his people to avoid the gaze of an older person or a superior. The circumstances of the encounter were awkward. But now things had changed. All of a sudden the two of them were to be his wives. Something like his father's. Perhaps in a not too distant future he would be able to say, "I have two white wives."

He concentrated on Roser. She was thin, but he could not figure out her age. Forty-something. Who knows? Maybe if he had lived in Catalonia for a longer time and he knew the people better, he would have known that Roser had the typical figure of an authentic Catalan woman: a slim, angular face, almost triangular, with certain male features, and a chin that looked like a bird's beak. Her hair was short and reddish. She had a nice figure, good-looking legs. She was not very pretty. But she wasn't ugly either. For his taste she was about average. He couldn't yet determine if she was friendly or unfriendly. Until that moment her laugh had seemed somewhat forced.

Montse was different. By the same token, if he had a good understanding of the different peoples of Spain, he would have realized that she was a pure hybrid—a mix of Valencia and Andalusia: a round face with a sweet expression and an easy, sincere smile. Her dark, shoulder-length hair highlighted the Andalusian and Valencian origins of her mother. She was a bit round, with prominent breasts that stood out beneath the knitted sweater she was wearing.

"Fine, Bambara Keita, now that we know each other better, let's make a few things clear." Montse accompanied her words with a few pats on his leg. "You know that we in Europe live a certain way. People in Europe are not free like they are in Africa. Do you know what I'm trying to say?"

"Yes, Europe good. Africa no. Africa much dictatorship, people not be free. No work for young. Dictatorship, bad presidents, stealing money. Corruption. No, Africa very bad."

The African had become indignant as he spoke of the situation on his continent. While Africans like to prove themselves worthy, they also love to denigrate where they're from. That was normal. In a land that only presented bad news to the world, how could the young speak well of it. However, as they speak badly about their land, no one seems to ask what they can do about it.

Bambara Keita followed that example. He found himself talking about combatting the scarcities that sent him into exile and all the bad things about Africa. He called the presidents crooks. But he did not talk about how he got a job in his district's post office despite not finishing his last year of secondary school. He landed that job through the lover of one of his sisters, who happened to be the director of the post office. For over a year many people did not receive their money orders. The same thing happened with other valuable packages from the interior. Only when his sister's lover was reassigned to another district did Bambara Keita and his friend lose their influence, and the new director fired them. Some people in his country could not figure out how the two of them did not end up in jail. But each time he recalled this incident in his life, he found no fault with what he did. The big fish rob much more, he told himself.

"Well, it's true that Africa has dictatorships, but that's not the kind of freedom I'm talking about."

Bambara Keita did not let his interlocutor finish. He was about to continue his harangue but Montse interrupted him with a smile.

"Look, what I want to tell you is that here people are different." She paused. She didn't know how to explain what she wanted him to understand. "People here for example cannot understand that a person like you—" She cut herself off again. "I mean a person of color like you, and me... how we can have relations..."

"Oh, yes. You mean that whites here are racists and no want Blacks to marry whites?"

"Something like that," affirmed Montse, slightly relieved.

"Ah, I know. In Africa too; mamás and papás no want their sons to marry whites."

"That's too much!" Roser was also indignant.

The African did not exactly understand Roser's expression.

"That no important. Blacks marry whites and whites marry Blacks. Not here in Barcelona. We all one world now."

"That's it." Montse got back into the conversation. "Despite all that, things are still difficult, complicated. What I want to say is that Roser and I are well known here. Our families are important, and as I said, people can be closed minded, not like in..." She was going to say Africa, but she did not finish the sentence. The native from there had just informed her that people in Africa are not so open-minded.

"We've got to be very careful."

She paused again. She looked at Bambara Keita. He was interested in what she was saying. He thought he knew what she was driving at.

"I do what you want," he said to relieve her discomfort.

This was the phrase Montse was hoping he would say.

"Well what we want of you is easy. We want discretion. For example if you see one of us in the street with other people, you have to pretend you don't know us. Just pass us by."

"I no say hello?"

"No!" Roser interrupted, almost screaming.

"Look," Montse began with a little less drama, "we'll see each other both here and at my place. When we're not here or at my place we'll feign we don't know each other. Eventually, I'm sure I'll tell my family that you're my butler..."

"What is butler?"

"Someone who works in my house. You help me with household duties a few days a week. If someone comes in when you're there, I'll tell you, for example, 'Bambara Keita, bring me a glass of water...' And you bring me the water. I'll show you how to serve it."

"The same goes for my place," Roser was quick to point out.

"That's it," confirmed Montse. "When we are with people, you should always address me as 'Señora,' never our first names. Do you understand?"

"Oh, yes! My father say goat eats where he's tied."

"What does that mean?" asked Roser.

"Means that I tied to you. I eat tied to you, I do all you want or ask."

"That saying is much better. I like it. That's just what you have to do." Roser was feeling better.

"Very well, Bambara Keita, I expect we'll do many good things together! Roser, we should celebrate with a bottle of Cava—what do you think?"

"A great idea," affirmed Roser as she stood up and happily headed toward the kitchen.

The host uncorked the bottle and filled the glasses; they all lifted their glasses and toasted. As they drank, they discussed other details of the project. Around eight o'clock Montse went home, leaving Bambara Keita alone with Roser, who would begin their experiment that very night. At the elevator Montse bade Roser farewell and whispered, "Let's get on with this. You'll see how well it all turns out."

She did not wait for a reply. She shut the elevator door and pressed the button for the ground floor.

CHAPTER 5

ROSER FORCED HERSELF TO BE friendly. She knew the African was uncomfortable. Until then they had always been in Montse's presence. It was her friend who knew the ins and outs of the new area they had entered.

Bambara Keita had registered her absence. He was a little less enthusiastic. Roser turned on the TV and the two of them sat down to watch. They had dinner around ten. Bambara Keita helped clear the table. Later Roser told him they could go to bed now. The African got his bag and took out his toothbrush, brushed his teeth and washed his mouth. As he exited the bathroom Roser came into the hallway. The African froze.

Roser had put on a transparent bathrobe that allowed a view of a nightgown and matching panties.

His host pointed to her bedroom and entered.

"Come right in, don't be afraid," she encouraged the African. She tried to encourage herself as well.

Bambara Keita entered her space. He shivered a bit at finding himself in a woman's room like hers.

"Do you like my room?" asked Roser in a slightly coquettish tone.

"Yes, very beautiful! I no been in room like this."

"Well, you and I are going to share it. Take off your clothes, but first take this."

She offered him a package, which the African accepted.

"What this?"

"Birth control."

"Ah, I have very good ones for me," he said as he took out his own pack of condoms.

"You've got some too."

"Oh, yes, always!"

"Very good, you can take off your clothes and leave them on that chair."

She began to take off her nightclothes. Her back was facing the African. When she turned around, the man was already completely naked. When she saw him she screamed, "Noooooo!"

Bambara Keita, somewhat distracted, not knowing exactly what had happened, was startled.

"What?"

Roser was trembling. She was looking straight at the man's penis and she could not find the words. She had covered her mouth, realizing the commotion her scream might cause. She was petrified, her eyes wide open.

"What wrong, Roser?"

"It's... th... at... thing," she managed to let out, pointing to the African's penis.

"What wrong with that?" he asked again, having no idea what the woman was scared of.

"That!" She pointed at his member.

"You mean my *bangala*?" he asked, with a slight smile on his face.

"Holy God, I have never seen anything like that. That's what you call it?" Little by little she was coming out of her stupor.

"Yes, what wrong with him? No like?" the African inquired, touching his penis and playing with it.

When he touched it, it became erect, and Roser shuddered even more.

"I don't like it, it's too big. You look like a horse. I can't." She started to put her nighty back on.

"No worry, Roser. The girls in my village tell me my *bangala* very small."

"Is that what the girls in your town tell you?" she asked incredulously.

"Yes, they say so, they laugh at me. They bad!"

"If they tell you that, they are not bad, they're beasts. They're not human!"

"What beasts?"

"Nothing. I'm sorry, but I can't."

Roser left the bedroom and shut the door. She grabbed her cell phone and called Montse.

"Who have you brought to my house, Montse?" she asked as soon as she heard Montse's voice.

"What's wrong, Roser?"

"I'm asking, who do you think you've found?"

"What are you talking about? God, calm down, talk to me. I don't know what you're saying."

"I can't calm down. I'm talking about the boy you found for us."

"Is there something wrong with Bambara Keita?"

"Yes, there's something wrong with him. There is something wrong with his penis!" Roser could barely speak.

"What's wrong with his dick? Is he sick? Is it too small...?"

"It's too big!" She almost screamed the last word.

"That's good, isn't it?"

"No, Montse, what that guy has between his legs is not a penis, it's a monster. I swear I've never seen anything like it."

"Roser, you're exaggerating."

"I swear to God I'm not exaggerating! I'm still shaking. This is bad luck. I told you. Of all the Blacks in this city, you bring us an abnormal one." Roser was beside herself.

"Please calm down. I don't understand how a woman your age can react like this just because she saw a man's prick."

"Montse, what that guy has is not a penis, I repeat: it's a monster.

He's not going to penetrate me. I don't want him to tear up my vagina."

"For God's sake, Roser, don't say that. We've already made the deal!"

"Look, Montse, say what you want but that Black guy is not going to penetrate me. I don't want him to ruin me. That's just what would happen to my vagina if I let him make love with me. And on top of it all, he has the nerve to tell me that the girls in his town make fun of him because his thing is small." Montse could only laugh from the other side of the telephone, a laugh that made her friend laugh as well.

"Don't laugh, Montse, this is very serious. If I lived from my vagina and I allowed this guy to penetrate me, I'd be unemployed."

The two of them laughed once more.

"So, you see, the girls in his town aren't scared of him."

"I told him that those girls are mares and mules like him."

"You told him that? Poor guy!"

"Poor guy? You mean poor woman who dares to spread her legs for him! It's too late to throw him out. But tomorrow I'll tell him to leave."

"If my aunts were not here with me now, I'd come get him. That's why I let you go first."

Roser did not let her finish.

"The first and the last. This experiment is over!"

They hung up. She went into the kitchen and made herself a cup of coffee. As she sipped, she smoked a cigarette.

Bambara Keita was in the bedroom waiting. He was disconcerted. He did not understand exactly what had happened. Roser had fled from the bedroom because his *bangala* was big. How can a woman look for a man and then be scared of him because of his member? As he asked himself, he looked at his penis. He thought it was normal. He remembered a boy in his town that was going through his circumcision. He was about nine or ten years old. They had performed the ritual with other boys about his age. In the days it took for the wound to heal he went straight under a baobab tree with the other boys. Once there, they would perform the ritual: they would uncover themselves and then, taking the their penises in their hands, they would press them on the tree that was said to have mythical powers. As they heroically endured the pain, the boys chanted, "Baobab, I want my father to be as big and strong as you." Each boy would repeat this as he touched his still healing penis to the tree. Bambara Keita, just like any boy of his town, had heard that this was what was done, and he did it too.

He hadn't had any more problems with his penis until this moment. Well, it's also true that when he was studying in the city he had been with a prostitute. She was twice his age. The woman had not seen his penis. When he entered her, she could not stand it. She pushed him off forcefully as she screamed at him, "*Muf, muf*! Out, out!" Bambara Keita fell off the bed. He got up and looked at the woman, who was furious. Her ire increased when she discovered his penis, "Yu wan kil mi wok ting... Muf. Muf!" The woman had thrown his money back at him and pushed him out of her hut, cursing him in pidgin English.

Bambara Keita laughed remembering that incident. After all, it was not injurious. Among themselves, the youngsters say that's how prostitutes are sometimes. At their core, they're afraid.

Roser went into the bedroom. Bambara Keita was sitting on the bed. He had put on his condom. He got up as soon as he saw her come in. The sight of the woman gave his penis another boost. His body began to shiver.

"Tomorrow you have to leave. This deal is over."

"Please, I no want to hurt you!" begged the African.

"No way!" She would either make him sleep in the living room or the guest room. The only thing that kept her from sending him to the guest room was that she was in no mood to change the sheets.

"Go to sleep, but don't touch me." She showed the African his side of the bed.

She took off her robe and slipped into bed. Bambara Keita did the same. Roser turned off the light. On the other side of the room a blue light was shining in the dark.

Bambara Keita began to think about his misfortune. He asked himself why life was so unjust. Just when he thought he had gotten out of the hell he had lived in since he left his country six years ago, it all came tumbling down because of his *bangala*.

Roser had her back to him and was looking at the other side of the room. He was lying on his back looking at the ceiling. He contemplated the room illuminated by a dim blue light she had installed. He had never slept in a room like this. How could he lose it all now?

He looked over at his sleeping partner. She was at ease. Bambara Keita thought of some conversations he had had with his friends. Sometimes, they said, women say no when they really mean yes. Was this the case with this white woman? He wanted to see if it was true. He placed his hand on the woman's back. She reacted adversely, grabbing his hand to make sure he didn't touch her. This white woman was different. Her no really meant no.

He could do nothing about it. A wave of sadness and a sense of failure took over him. He wasn't blind. From the moment he arrived at that house he suspected that his host was not convinced that their plan was a good thing. He knew that if Roser were not in favor, the other one would not go through with it. Surely when she left the bedroom she was going to call Montse to tell her about his big prick, and then they would agree to throw him out. *My God, how can you put honey in front of my lips only to take it away from me? Your faithful servant, you know how much I need it,* he heard his heart ask his Master. He was on the verge of tears.

He closed his eyes. He suddenly recalled a children's tale an old storyteller from his village recounted under the moon. It was about a panther and a turtle. The two were friends and neighbors. One day their sons became ill. The two boys seemed to suffer from the same illness. It was a serious sickness, and none of the healers in town could do anything about it. So they sent for a sorcerer from a nearby village who aimed to figure out the cause of the sickness. To cure them, he told the two fathers to find a crocodile's tear in a river far from their village. It was a difficult river to find. That's what the other village dwellers thought. However, the two fathers, accepting the responsibility, set out to find the river. After nearly three days on their quest they finally found it. They saw many crocodiles floating on the surface of the water. They crouched down in the brush and waited.

"How will we be able to get one of their tears?" the turtle's father asked the panther's father.

"As soon as we see one of them get out of the water, I'll go after him. I'll give him a blow and then I'll bite him, and he'll cry," assured the panther.

"But it will be dangerous. He could kill you," warned the turtle.

"No crocodile on this earth can overtake me," the panther's father boasted.

The turtle kept on arguing that the panther's plan was impossible and instead tried to figure out one of his own. Then, at that very moment, an enormous crocodile emerged from the water. The panther seized the opportunity. With a stick in his paw, he pounced on the crocodile. The crocodile saw him coming and was prepared for his aggressor's challenge. The panther managed to strike a blow, but the crocodile bit the panther's leg. He lost three of his fingers. Crying and lamenting his misfortune, the panther went back home without even saying goodbye to the turtle.

Meanwhile, the turtle had stayed put in his hiding place—he saw it all happen from there. After the panther had left, he stood up with a plan in mind. He found a hollow bamboo branch. He gathered some of the leaves that looked like tobacco and ground them into a powder. He returned to his hiding place. Night was about to fall, and the crocodile went back into the water along with the other crocodiles. He waited until the next day. When the sun came up, the turtle saw the crocodile wade out of the water in search of the sun's rays. The turtle waited patiently for the sun to warm the old crocodile's thick skin.

Time passed. The turtle watched the crocodile's movements intently. After waiting for a long time, the father turtle saw that the crocodile had barely moved. He carefully moved his hollow bamboo stick out of the bushes and maneuvered it to the crocodile's nostril. Once the bamboo was nearly touching the crocodile's nose, the turtle blew into it. Unaware, the crocodile inhaled the powder and started to sneeze. The turtle then moved the bamboo to the crocodile's eye, and when he started to cry, one of his tears streamed into the bamboo pole. Slowly, the turtle retracted the bamboo and found the tear inside—he had captured it! He went back to his village, mixed the crocodile's tear with the herbs the healer had prescribed, and bathed his son in the mixture. His son recovered, while the panther's son died a few days later.

Bambara Keita thought about this story. He would not wait until the next day like the turtle. He did not have the luxury of time. But neither could he act impulsively like the panther. He had to go directly after his objective, patiently following the turtle's example. At the same time, he knew he had to be quick like the panther. So he waited, but not long. Soon he heard Roser's light snore as she slept. He got ready. He delicately moved the cover and sheet toward the foot of the bed. He contemplated Roser's exposed panties and negligee. He moved back to face her. He extended his right hand toward her panties and his left hand to her breasts. Slowly moving his fingers down toward her panties, he combined the movements of both of his hands: the fingers of his right hand slipped into her vagina, rubbing against her clitoris, as the other hand caressed one of her breasts.

His unexpected caresses nudged Roser out of her sleep. She shuddered. She did not have time to react. Her body tensed. The young man stroked her clitoris, increasing pressure on it. Roser groaned. Bambara Keita continued. Sensing that the woman was yielding, he became fully attentive to her. His hands still in contact with her sensitive parts, he felt the woman tremble. Her body had been in dire need of pleasure for a long time. From her mouth came several continuous groans.

Bambara Keita brought his lips to the woman's belly. He lifted her nighty and licked her skin. Removing her panties, he descended toward her pussy. He knelt down and placed his entire face between her legs. His tongue methodically traced the entrance to her vagina. As he nibbled at her clitoris, Roser looked as though she had left this world. She groaned again several times, begging him not to stop. Her body was grateful after years of having suffered the punishment of a sexually repressive society.

"Oh God, thank you!" she screamed in ecstasy.

The immigrant then traced her body, from her legs to her breasts, with his tongue. He gently bit her nipples through the nighty. The slight irritation produced another special pleasure in the native. Knowing now that she had let go, he moved his legs on top of hers and separated them. He took hold of his penis with one hand and caressed her clitoris with it. He penetrated her halfway and then took it out. The pleasure of those movements made her thighs tighten and welcome the hard flesh that had so terrified her. The young man did not want to go too fast, even though he knew she was well lubricated. He kept playing with her. In an unexpected movement, almost unconsciously, Roser thrust her legs upward. She spread them as wide as she could. She grabbed his hips and brusquely moved them toward her.

Bambara Keita, surprised, allowed her to lead him. He entered the woman's insides like a missile. Roser uttered a long, loud cry of pain. For a moment the man did not move. The woman cleaved to him, scratching his back with her fingernails.

"Ayyy!" he cried out to her.

Not even that cry could make her loosen her grip. She was at the verge of fainting. The two of them endured the pain in a firm embrace. Roser stopped scratching her lover's back, but she continued to wrap her arms around him. Now feeling less confined, Bambara Keita tried to move.

"No, please, don't move!" she begged in a barely audible voice.

He obeyed. From that position, he licked her neck, then her ear. Slowly he moved his hips, slipping his prick gradually out and then back in. That movement gave her as much pain as pleasure, as she continued to let out cries of delightful anguish. It was at that very point of convergence that Roser experienced one of many orgasms.

With time, the man was able to withdraw his penis and thrust it in with greater ease. It took so long that an hour and a half later he could no longer contain himself. He emptied himself in the midst of screams and jolts of their two bodies. Finally, they were still, he on top of her. Ten minutes later, he withdrew his penis, carefully holding the condom in place.

"That door over there is to the bathroom," he heard her say softly. "The light switch is on the wall on the left, if you need to use it."

Bambara Keita got out of bed and went over to the bathroom. He turned on the light and shut the door quietly behind him. This bathroom was enormous, with jars of lotions and perfumes of all kinds everywhere. As soon as he entered, he saw a wide mirror hanging on the wall. He looked at himself. He had never seen himself as whole and natural as in that image. He smiled. The mirror showed his white teeth. "I have entered paradise," he murmured to himself. The story of the panther, the turtle, and the crocodile had proved instructive. He had used the wisdom and patience of the turtle, combined with the agility of the panther.

He looked at his sex. The condom was tinted with blood and thick sperm dripped from his member. He tore off a strip of tissue next to the commode and wiped himself as he took off his condom. He threw it in the trashcan. How would he wash himself? There was a bidet whose use he did not know. He tiptoed over and held his penis over the sink. Would he wet the floor? He did not think any more about it. He went into the shower stall and this time he knew to close the door. When he finished he went back to bed. His companion did not move. She remained in bed as he had left her, naked and uncovered. He covered her and got back under the sheets. He placed his hand on her breast and left it there. As he caressed her, he fell asleep.

When Roser discovered he was sleeping, she carefully took his hand off her body and tried to get up. She tried to leave quickly but she slowed down when she felt a pain between her legs. She balanced herself by holding onto the night table. It was difficult to get to the bathroom. Once she was there she managed to sit down over the bidet. She peed and saw that her urine had a red tint. It stung but she managed to empty her bladder. When it had gone down the drain, she turned on the faucets.

Roser felt the cold water penetrate her deeply. She stayed that way for a long while, motionless until she felt comfortable. Then she reached for a small jar of Betadine on one of the glass shelves. She mixed a few drops of the disinfectant with water from the sink.

She went back to bed about an hour later, feeling much better. Before falling back into bed she observed her companion. Bambara Keita was sleeping peacefully and breathing softly. His ebony face blended with the navy blue color of the sheets. He looked like a child. He was a child, thought Roser. A thirty-three-year-old child. A marvelous child!

Roser tenderly ran her hand through his hair. Sometimes life is good! Why was there so much suffering and discrimination? Life should be how it was for her at that moment: pure pleasure.

She turned on a small lamp on the night table. She caressed the young man's face. Bambara Keita opened his eyes.

"Hola."

"Hola," he replied.

They lay there looking at each other for a while without saying anything.

"Please, please put a condom back on and make love to me with all your might like you did before. I need it! I need you!"

The man smiled. From the position he was in he extended his hand toward the night table and grabbed the package of condoms. Their bodies met. This time with less pain. Roser squirmed with pleasure. They changed positions. She climbed on top of him and rode him like an Amazon. It took a bit longer than the first time. When they separated, Bambara Keita sank into the bed. He covered himself without getting up to take off his condom. Roser turned to him. She embraced him, and they both went to sleep.

The telephone rang. Roser woke up, but she could barely open her eyes. Lazily, she grabbed the phone on the night table.

"Yes?"

It was Montse. "Roser, excuse me, I'm running late. I'll be there before eleven."

"For God's sake, Montse, it's way too early to call!"

"It's nine thirty, but as I said, I'll be there right away."

"No hurry, it's early."

"What? What have you done with him?"

"Nothing."

"Where is he?"

"He's right here, sleeping."

"I don't understand. I don't understand what you're saying."

"Don't worry. Start making lunch, I'll bring him to you just like we planned."

She did not wait for Montse's reply. She hung up, and immediately took the phone off the hook.

CHAPTER 6

*F*ROM THE KITCHEN, MONTSE HEARD someone at her door. She interrupted what she was doing, washed her hands, dried them with her apron, and went to the door. Before she opened it, she hesitated a few seconds in front of the hallway mirror and looked at herself. She touched up her hair and makeup. When she was satisfied, she opened the door. It was Roser and Bambara Keita. As they came in, she looked up and down the outside hallway, to make sure no one had seen them in the adjacent apartments.

"Well, hi there, you happy couple."

"Hola," replied the African.

Roser did not respond. She seemed tired. She went directly to the couch and plunged into the cushions.

"God, that was good," she sighed.

Montse looked at her. Roser's eyes were hidden behind sunglasses. Bambara Keita stood, not knowing exactly what to do. Montse noticed his discomfort.

"Sit down here, Bambara Keita!"

The African obeyed. Montse observed him. He was wearing the same jacket as the day before, but his disposition was different. Something had changed in him since yesterday; she could not figure out exactly what. His face, of course, was the same—or almost the same, because the dark eyes she had seen yesterday had taken on a certain shine. His cheeks were also different, a bit sunken, not as full. But this might be due to the young man's slimness. There was something about him that Montse could not put her finger on.

She did not waste time trying to figure all this out. She decided that the young man was even better looking than she thought. This conclusion excited her. She looked over at her friend. Roser remained in a daze. She was falling asleep.

"Well, let me step back into the kitchen. I've got something cooking."

They paid no mind as Montse disappeared. Bambara Keita stayed in the living room with Roser. He looked around. While Roser's apartment was impressive, Montse's was exceptionally so. Everything was decorated with exquisite taste. The paintings on the wall were beautiful, even though he did not like the drawings. His knowledge of art was minimal. What could he know about Miró or Picasso? Everything was marvelous, but for the most part, these paintings did not say anything to him. There was one he liked. It was a nude woman with prominent breasts, leaning outside on a windowsill and staring into the horizon nostalgically.

The African turned from his inspection of the house to his companion. Roser was still motionless, sitting in her chair. She was exhausted, as was Bambara Keita. Montse didn't know how to read his tired, albeit relaxed, face. Of course he was both tired and relaxed. He had gotten up at ten thirty for breakfast. He had drunk about a liter of milk accompanied by who knows how many pieces of toast. And as he finished his breakfast he felt Roser's hand between his legs.

"Are you too tired to make love again, sweetness?" he heard her ask.

He would have liked to say he was beat, but he was in no condition to show weakness on his first day of work. So, as he did often, he just nodded his head. He then went for one of his special condoms. He put it on and headed to the bedroom, but Roser had him pick up something in the kitchen so that he would follow. She felt his body against her back, his hands on her breasts. She turned around and gave him a wet kiss. The man picked her up and placed her on the kitchen counter. With her legs spread and her back to the marble tiles, he penetrated her, minus the delicacy of the first two times.

"Ay!" she cried, again with pain and pleasure.

Bambara Keita was beside himself, focusing on the insertion and removal of his prick in the woman's vagina. Roser, for her part, did not stop groaning lustfully.

Bambara Keita had never made love that way to a Black woman. The women he knew did not have kitchens as elaborate as this one, with such large counters. But he had seen how they had used them in the movies, so he imitated those movements. And what a unique sex position it was! It was exciting for him. He pretended to be a movie actor. He abruptly pulled his dick out of her. She was stunned, crying out desperately. As she looked at him with eyes of wonderment, he put his arms around her.

"Come here," he said calmly.

He lifted her off the counter. Roser thought he was leading her to the bedroom. He made her turn around and lean over the counter where she had just been sitting. Roser allowed him to take the lead. She obeyed her lover like an automaton. With her head and arms resting on the cold marble counter, the man straightened her legs and spread them. Roser had no time to think. At once she felt his hardness enter her deepest reaches.

"Déu meu!" she screamed.

The African felt delight at her pleasure. He did not give his lover a break. Nor did he care about the pain his huge rod might be causing. Roser was losing her balance. She tried to lift her head and stand up. It was impossible. Her lover was holding her so tight that he made her double over. She fell to the kitchen floor with him on top of her, and there they kept moving like two beasts. When they were finished, the man rolled over, resting his back on the tiles without caring how cold they were. Roser did not move. She lay face down. Again, they were both exhausted. They looked at the clock, it was one in the afternoon. He washed himself. She got dressed, and a few minutes later they were ready for their meeting with Montse, feeling utterly spent.

Montse was in the kitchen, filled with curiosity about what her friend had done with their African. She had no idea that the two had surrendered to each other. She could no longer stand it, so she went into the living room.

"Roser, can you help me?"

Her friend got up and sleepily walked into the kitchen. As soon as she got there she collapsed onto the first chair she could find.

"Girl, it looks like you've been run over by a train."

"Worse than that. I'm in pieces, I can't even feel my insides."

"A big difference, no?"

"Please, no comments or questions," she begged.

"Well, that'll be hard for me to do. Last night you were on the verge of throwing the guy onto the street, and today everything's changed. Honestly, I'm pleased."

"Yes, like you say, I was about to throw him out. But you stopped me. I took your advice, and things just happened."

"For the better, I hope." Montse was laughing.

"I don't know if it's for the better. All I know is that my body no longer feels like it's mine."

"Maybe you went too far."

"That young man is an animal, a real sex machine."

"You mean he is or you are?"

"I admit that I was in need. Luckily he had his own birth control. He told me he got them in a pharmacy that a whore had recommended, in the rough part of town.

"Really?"

"That's what he told me when I asked him this morning. We were lucky because the ones I have don't fit. I think his were a German brand," informed Roser.

"So does that mean German men have bigger dicks than our guys?"

"Maybe so. Remember when it was hard to find large sized shoes for women in Spain, and in Germany you could find up to size 10 and bigger? They are always ahead of us!"

"Let's try to find the brand, then. We'll order half a ton of them if necessary." Montse laughed at herself, then added, "I suppose that you haven't used up all the condoms. I hope you left some for me. You better not have finished them."

"There are enough condoms. And as far as he is concerned, I promise you he's healthy. But let's make sure we don't feed him too much, because the result might be disastrous for us."

"If we don't feed him, we'll kill him."

"I'm just saying, we were together the whole night. This morning after drinking over a liter of milk and eating everything I put in front of him, he took me like a wild colt. It was as good as the first time. Really, we need to be careful not to feed him too much."

"We'll see. Now, let's eat."

"As soon as we finish, I'm leaving. I need some sleep."

"I certainly won't be the one to keep you. Just remember to take the spare key to my place and come by tomorrow morning to fetch him. As I told you, I need to leave early and I don't want to wake him up at that hour, poor guy. But we need to be careful. If he goes down the stairs or takes the elevator alone, the doorman or neighbors will ask questions. And he can't be asleep in the apartment when the cleaning lady comes. Let's not attract any comments or scandals. I will need time to spread the rumor that I'm sharing my place with an employee and his girlfriend."

"Don't worry. I'll be here on time. But at least make sure your alarm clock is on so that he can wash in the morning. Because from what I've seen he really likes to wash himself. For whatever reason, he's always in the bathroom making sure he's clean," added Roser.

They brought the plates of food into the dining room. Bambara Keita was a bit more sure of himself than he had been the previous day. He ate everything they put on his plate. Montse had made a garbanzo bean stew, and she filled his plate to the brim.

"Eat! You're very thin. A man your height needs to have more flesh on his bones. Garbanzos are good for that!" Roser gave her a look, but Montse did not pay attention. They washed down their meal with a bottle of wine from Navarra. Bambara Keita thought it was a bit sweet, but it was certainly better than the wine they had had yesterday. Still, he thought the wine that rich white people drank was strange. The wine he was used to went down more easily. But that was where the poor people lived—he was now among the elite, the rich! When he was in Africa he thought that in European countries there was no such thing as rich and poor. Who would have thought!

Bambara Keita was satisfied after the first dish. He had eaten a lot, thinking that this first helping would be the only one. But he had to be careful dealing with these whites and their tendency to serve two, three, or even four courses of food in one sitting. He should have known.

Montse served him a plate of two thick steaks. *How the hell can I eat this?* he asked himself.

"Meat is very nourishing, and it's healthy," commented Montse.

"Oh, yes, but I eat too much," the African protested.

"What are you talking about? You're young and you need to be strong."

Roser gave her another look, and then said softly to Montse, "Just hope that this food winds up in other parts of his body, and not down—"

"You're too much!" Montse mocked her friend.

They were speaking in Catalan and their guest did not understand. Roser just shrugged her shoulders, and they kept on eating. Bambara Keita, who was a strong believer, was loyal to his doctrine that one should never throw anything away. So he ate everything, even dessert.

After a cigarette, Roser said, "I'll help clear, and then I'm gone."

"Don't worry about it. Bambara Keita and I will clean up. Right, Bambara Keita?"

"Oh, yes."

"Well I won't insist," said Roser as she stood up. "I'm leaving. Goodbye, see you tomorrow."

Montse and Bambara Keita cleared the table where they had just eaten. When he got to the kitchen, the African approached the counter with the intention of washing the dishes.

"What are you going to do?"

"Wash dishes."

"No, Bambara Keita, don't do that. That is not your work. Your responsibility in this house is of a different kind," she declared as she approached him and gave him a kiss. "I have a cleaning lady who comes by three times a week. Besides, she doesn't wash the dishes by hand. That machine over there is for washing dishes."

Bambara Keita had already seen such a machine at Roser's place, where he had tried to do the same.

"Well, if someone comes in unexpectedly, I can tell you, 'Bambara Keita, put those dishes in the dishwasher,' and you'll do it. You put them in like this." She showed him how. "The visitor could be my mother, one of my aunts, or a friend. You know how curious we women are. I'm sure that they'll want to come and see a man work in the kitchen because here men don't do that customarily. So you just do as you wish, like I've shown you."

After an impromptu lesson, they went into the dining room.

"What if we take a little nap?" she suggested, and left the kitchen.

Bambara Keita, despite having been at his new job for a relatively short time, knew that was an order disguised as a question.

"Oh, yes, fine!"

From the bathroom Montse called him, "Look at the toothbrush and toothpaste I bought you."

Then she herself started brushing her teeth. Bambara Keita was pleased by the gesture. Roser had not done this the whole time he had been at her place. When they got out of bed, she wobbled over to the kitchen and they had breakfast.

He, on the other hand, had gotten out his toothbrush and paste.

"I have this in bag."

"It doesn't matter. Use this one, it's newer," she said affably.

When they finished, Montse grabbed his hand and took him to the bedroom. When they went in, the African was stupefied. The room was very large and well-decorated. Bambara Keita suddenly realized the differences between the two women who had hired him. Montse not only attended to her teeth with greater care, but she was also more orderly. Everything in her house was well placed. If Roser's place impressed him, this one did so even more.

"Nice."

"Do you like it?"

"Oh, yes, very nice," said the African as he looked over the entire room.

"Thank you. I'm pleased you like it, because from now on this room is yours, too. The whole apartment is."

She opened the curtains. Bambara Keita kept admiring the room. He felt great pride inside him. What a life! Who would have told him that he could lie down in a bed like that with a woman of such class? If only his father, mother, and all his relatives could see him! They would be so proud. And if his neighbors in his town or even those he had met in the city peeked into that room and saw him... Too bad that he was so far away from them!

Montse slipped under the covers, where she proceeded to undress. She did not exactly have a figure to boast about, this she knew. Despite the fact that she was in the company of a hired hand, willing to do anything she wanted, she preferred to do what she would do with any lover. That was respectable behavior. She held out her hand.

"Come here, love."

Her voice sounded soft to him. The African did not make her beg. He took the hand she had extended; the other one coaxed him closer to the bed.

"First, sit here."

Bambara Keita obeyed. He sat down. As soon as he did so, she moved her mouth close to his. She kissed him passionately. The African felt her tongue delve greedily into his mouth. His mouth opened more widely and his thick lips pressed forcefully against the woman's.

Bambara Keita brought his hand to the breasts of his lover and employer. They were enormous. Not even both of his hands could cover one of them completely. Montse became more excited when she felt the man's hand on her. She grabbed his head and pressed it into her breasts. She held him so tightly that he could barely breathe.. He resisted. Montse realized that she was suffocating him. She let go of his head so that the African could take some breaths.

But she did not retreat. From his head she moved her hands to collar of his jacket and began to take it off. She threw it away from the bed. Then she put her arms around her lover's trunk and drew him close to her, and said, "Come to your Montse!"

Bambara Keita had no time to think. The woman drew him toward her so violently that by the time he realized what was happening, he found himself on top of her. Montse moved the sheets to one side so that she could feel the man's skin touching hers.

The African was now able to take in the full view of her enormous body and tantalizingly soft skin. Her bare breasts were the largest he had ever contemplated from so close. They were also the most delicious and exciting. He pressed his lips greedily against her nipples, moving from one to the other. Then he buried his head between them without her coaxing. His movements seemed to transport his lover-boss away from this world, launching her into the next, a world of pleasure.

Again he noticed the difference between the two women. Montse's velvety, sweet-smelling skin excited him. Roser was thin, and her skin was dry, a bit rough and freckled. Montse's was all silk.

"I put condom," he declared lifting his head up from her breasts.

"Yes, love! But please be quick, your Montse is burning!"

Bambara Keita left the bedroom to fetch his bag. He did not take long. When he got back he already had it on, but he wore his pants. He had had a bad experience at first with Roser, and he did not want to repeat it. While Roser ended up surrendering to him, he could not be sure the other one would do the same.

"Aren't there any condoms left?" There was a slightly worried expression on the native's face.

Assenting, he pointed between his legs to indicate that he already had it on.

He moved toward her, then let himself fall on her. He did not want her to see his penis before he entered her. They both employed the same tactic. Montse avoided the possible shock of her first glance at his package, and he, in turn, tried to hide the size of his cock before the moment of penetration.

Montse received him with open arms. Bambara Keita kissed her with delight. The strong odor of smoke and metal emanating from a few of Roser's false teeth had deprived him of sexual pleasure. Montse was different. Her teeth were all white, clean, and healthy, not yellowish like her friend's. Her breath was soft, exciting. Despite the woman's exorbitant size, Bambara Keita told himself that he had definitely entered paradise. He savored the woman's mouth. He moved back toward her nipples and got deeper under the sheets. He slid to her side so that he could move his hand between her legs. He had a hard time finding the entrance to her vagina. When he finally found it, he slid his finger inside. The touch electrified the woman's entire body.

Montse coaxed him to move on top of her. She was plump and strong, while he was slim. Once he was on top, Montse started to pull down his pants. Bambara Keita helped her. Now completely naked, he tried to penetrate her. It was not easy. Each time she tried to spread her legs, she found that her thighs were accustomed to rubbing against one another. They seemed stuck together.

"Wait, my love."

Montse wanted to quash her thighs' rebellion. She pushed the man to one side of the bed. She crouched down with her legs apart. Bambara Keita came at her from behind. An enormous rear end was waiting for him, just when she invited him to possess her. His prick got even harder when he contemplated the lips of the woman's exposed pussy. He entered her, even though the position was a bit uncomfortable for him. He did this with such excitement that the woman screamed and fell flat on the bed, with him still inside her. He realized then that his motion had been cruel. The two lay there breathing heavily without moving. Montse felt an intense pain that seemed to paralyze her body. It was as if someone had shoved a thick iron rod up her vagina. She could barely believe what had just entered her was a human penis. It had been a mistake not to look at first. Her mind turned to the conversation she had had with Roser the previous night. Hell! What did this baby face have between his legs? Were all the years absent from his boyish face concentrated in his dick? Roser had told her he was a monster. Now that she had experienced it, she was convinced that Roser was right, or maybe worse. Because only something monstrous—much more than just a penis—could have produced such intense pain. The aching did not allow her to move. She sensed his huge member reached her stomach, maybe even her throat.

She lay there not knowing how to react. How to parse what was paralyzing her—had pain or pleasure burned her body? She felt overwhelmed, perhaps even defeated. So she waited.

Bambara Keita also had difficulty seeing the situation as a positive one. *God, this woman's ass is just too big! It looks like a mountain.* He tried not to move so as not to hurt her, as he thought he might be doing. But that mountain of a butt would not allow him to get comfortable.

As he thought about how to proceed, Montse began to show signs of life. She tried to move, little by little. It was difficult but she had no choice. Slowly she managed to lift her butt up. That heroic attempt involved a series of little movements that had the effect of exciting them both. Bambara Keita rose to the occasion. He slipped his penis out slowly, then reentered equally slowly. At first it was not easy. Montse's butt did not give him much leeway to move with pleasure and comfort. But he told himself it was a matter of time. He adjusted to Montse's dimensions. And little by little, Montse's painful sighs turned into sighs of pleasure. Now they were in unison. She slowly got back into her earlier position. Her orgasms followed one by one, accompanied at times by inaudible expressions. She was a bit uncomfortable but she remedied this by propping herself up on a pillow.

Bambara Keita also wanted to show he was a worthy lover, and that he deserved the role offered to him. The extreme size of his dick aided him in this endeavor. Under the circumstances, no other human being could have satisfied his lover-boss while satisfying himself at the same time. But he could do it. He did all he could to feel at ease while fulfilling his responsibility.

As he did with Roser, he pulled out his rod with no warning. A sound of disappointment came from the woman's mouth. But she did not have much time to complain, because the lover- employee, taken by his own desire, placed his mouth and his entire face under her butt. He sucked her thick vaginal lips, her behind covering his entire face.

"Dear God, I'm dying!"

Montse cried as she reached orgasm, the first of many. With his face covered in blood-tinged vaginal fluid, his nose and mouth smelling of pussy and ass, he took his head out from under the legs of his lover-boss and asked her to change positions. Boldly he decided to take her from the top. The woman didn't resist. Just the opposite, she was thankful. To go back to the missionary position comforted her and allowed her more energy to continue her enjoyment. Overcoming his initial nervousness, the man managed to penetrate her, although not without difficulty. It was a triumph that Montse again thanked him for. She had sure as hell made a good choice in a lover. It was worth it!

When, an hour later, they had both emptied themselves, he lay on top of her as if he were floating on an inner tube in a swimming pool. She stroked his hair with maternal tenderness.

"Please don't move, stay on top of me!" she begged when he made a slight movement.

Bambara Keita, exhausted, obeyed. The only move he made was to place his head between her tits as best he could. A few minutes later he started to snore. But the snoring didn't bother Montse. On the contrary, the snores filled her with tender joy as she continued to run her hands through his hair.

She also fell asleep. When she opened her eyes, Bambara Keita was still sleeping next to her. It had gotten dark outside. She turned on the lamp. It was seven o'clock. She moved the sheets and bedspread to one side. She wanted to get up. Her legs were hurting her, as well as her vagina and her entire lower body, even her breasts. She had to get to the bathroom. Sliding to one side, she managed to get her top half off the bed. She then placed one hand on the floor and took one leg out of the bed, and then the other. She tried not to make any noise, so as not to awaken her man.

Just as Roser had struggled to reach the bathroom, likewise Montse had to crawl on all fours. When she got there she climbed into the bathtub, but not without difficulty. She turned on the faucets, and as the water flowed she began to regain alertness. She turned the hot water on first, then gradually added the cold to reach the proper temperature, allowing the perfectly tepid water to fill her vagina. She soaked in the tub for nearly an hour. When she got out she felt better. At least she could stand up. Once again, Mother Nature's clean water had performed a miracle.

After drying herself and applying body lotion, she went back to bed, this time supporting herself by leaning on the walls. Bambara Keita woke up. They began a conversation. They barely had anything worth talking about. Mostly Montse asked questions about Africa, and Bambara Keita replied with short answers, above all when it had to do with his own country, Mali. By nine, they were hungry. Montse could very well have sent him to the kitchen to make them something to eat. But she realized that he would have no idea how to turn on the stove or work the microwave. When he got out of bed he headed to the bathroom. She took some cured meats out of the refrigerator and put them on the table, and when he came out of the bathroom, they ate dinner. They went back to bed at eleven.

The bath and the dinner gave them energy. They began to touch, caress, and kiss each other again. Montse knelt down on the bed beside him.

"Love, put it in me again, and don't worry even if I tell you it hurts."

Bambara Keita was surprised at her boldness. But he was there to obey, not to think or react to her orders. As he thought about his obligation, he remembered an incident from his childhood, when he had accompanied his grandfather on a hunt. It was the first time he had done so. He was only thirteen years old. Until then he had been happy playing with friends his own age. Rather than hunting, they set traps in the trees for squirrels and birds. Every now and then they ran after wild rats with spears.

He barely slept the night before, thinking about the adventure his grandfather had promised. His grandfather gave him a real spear with a wooden handle and a pointed iron head. As they went deeper into the jungle, the two dogs accompanying them saw a porcupine and ran after it. Grandfather and grandson ran off behind the dogs. The old man was still strong, but he was getting old and feeling pain in his joints. Bambara Keita passed his grandfather and arrived quickly where the dogs had surrounded the porcupine. In defense, the porcupine had lowered his head, releasing its spines, in defense. The dogs, knowing instinctively the danger of the spines, kept their distance, but they would not allow the porcupine to escape.

Bambara Keita, hoping for a success on his first hunting adventure, threw the spear with all his might toward the ball of spines. Bull's-eye. The porcupine fell on its back. The two dogs approached to make sure the animal was dead. But for some reason he was concerned for the safety of the dogs. Was it because the wounded animal continued thrashing violently, defending himself? Was it because he wanted to show his grandfather that he was a man? Or did it have to do with his inexperience? He grabbed a stick and hit the dogs to make them run off. And sure enough, they did so, squealing. Free now of the dogs, Bambara Keita got close to his prey and watched it squirm. The spear had penetrated one of its thighs. He raised the wooden handle of the spear as the animal continued twisting and contorting, somehow causing the pointed head of the lance to fall out. The porcupine, seeing that it was free, although still bleeding, summoned all its strength and ran off. "Look out, he's getting away!" the boy heard his grandfather warn. But the warning came too late.

Too late. Bambara Keita threw his machete to the ground. It immediately hid between some nearby rocks. The dogs came back to help their master, forgiving him for the hurt and humiliation he had caused them just a few minutes ago. They went to the rocks where the porcupine was hiding, drooling and barking, anxious to continue the hunt. But it was all in vain.

Bambara Keita could not live down this failure, not that day nor throughout his entire life. Porcupine meat was a delicacy among his people for its taste, and prized for its skin. And not only did his first attempt—an attempt that, if successful, would have turned him into a real hunter—end in failure, but to make it all worse, neither he nor his grandfather were able to catch anything for the rest of the morning. They returned with empty arms. His grandfather, seeing Bambara Keita so dispirited, sat down on his bamboo mat in the House of the Word and told him a story about a war between two communities of animals, in which the losers fell simply because they had sung their victory prematurely. Bambara Keita, despite his young age, understood his grandfather's story as a warning against the danger of overconfidence. Too much of it can be a bad thing. He should not have assumed success without first assuring that his prey lay dead in the leather bag he had brought just for that purpose.

"You made several mistakes. The worst one was to shoo away the dogs," his grandfather had told him, and that was the end of that.

All those images passed through his mind in a matter of moments, moments that seemed like an eternity to his lover-boss who awaited him, absolutely oblivious to his memories.

"My love, put it in me, please, don't worry about me, I'll be fine," she ordered and begged at once.

Bambara Keita emerged from the jungle of his youth and back into the luxurious bedroom in Barcelona. After that imaginary trip, what remained on his mind was the debacle of the porcupine and the moral of his grandfather's story. He must not allow himself to fail. That is why he should not be weak or overconfident. He must make sure his job is well done. His prey must be in the sack. Considering the initial impression his *bangala* had made due to its size, he could have lost his job. But now he realized it could turn out to be a valuable instrument for his work. He was discovering that the possible pain his shaft might cause his lover could also be the source of great pleasure. He had to finish the job, and do it well. "Don't worry about me, nothing will happen." Montse's words echoed in his ears.

Thus he was determined to complete his task with as much efficiency as possible. Before him was Montse's enormous ass. He found the lips of her pussy and separated them softly as he introduced the head of his penis. After assuring that his penis was steady and inside of her, he grabbed her behind and backed up a little. He braced himself and thrust forward with all his might. Montse felt like something meteoric was entering her and ripping at her insides. From her throat came a howl that might have come from something non-human.

"Dead...!", Bambara Keita cried in his native language, harmonizing with his lover-boss's animal scream. When she came back to reality, Montse found herself inert, face down on the bed with the African on top of her.

Montse showed no signs of life. Her face was covered in tears, but the man could not see them. Bambara Keita felt her breathe, so he knew she was still alive, although surely wounded. He thought perhaps he had gone too far in completing his task. He was motionless with his prick inside her, awaiting her orders.

Montse did not move. She did not want to. For a moment the pleasure had ceased. She felt only pain. But fortunately that was short lived. In her state of semi-consciousness, she began to feel the intensity of her pain in proportion to her pleasure. That experience encouraged her. It emboldened her.

She didn't move for several minutes, as she considered coming back to life, to continue. She made sure the sensation of pain did not surpass that of pleasure. She tried to move her legs. First, only the left one. It was not a major move, but it was something. She did the same with the right, and she was equally successful. Now that her legs could move, she tried to move her ass, but she had to be very careful. A false move could be incorrectly interpreted by her companion; he might think that she wanted him to do it again. She couldn't speak. She didn't want to. She did not know exactly why. Was it that she was not able, or that she did not wish to? Was she angry at her lover-employee, resentful for all the damage he had caused? Or was her silence coming from her wish not to let anyone know she was crying. Because she knew she was crying. The intense pain was making her cry despite the pleasure. Perhaps experiencing both sensations at the same time was causing the tears.

In the meantime, she thought she could continue to use his body to send out messages. She began to move her enormous butt slowly over his body from one side to the other, left then right.

Bambara Keita understood that she was recuperating. He was still waiting for orders. With time these orders arrived and he knew how to interpret them. Now Montse began to move her ass up and down. When she did so a few times, the African read it as a signal that he could again get down to work. He began to move with her, at first gently. Soon Montse's groans filled the bedroom, breaking the silence of a few moments earlier.

Bambara Keita was fulfilling the woman's wish. One orgasm came after another. It went on longer than before. An extraordinary sense of well-being had overcome the lovers. Montse had experienced the most sexual pleasure of her entire life, and Bambara Keita was satisfied and proud for having completed his task and having done it well. Relaxed and exhausted, they both fell asleep.

Montse was awakened by the bedside light. Someone had turned it on. It was Roser.

"I thought you had a meeting."

"What time is it?" Montse was a little annoyed.

"It's eight."

"I didn't go, I can't even get up."

"What are you going to do?"

"I'll call my secretary and tell her I'm not well." She tried to get up. "Please give me a hand, help me get up."

Roser helped her put on her bathrobe, as Montse leaned on her to proceed to the kitchen.

"I'm going to make you some coffee."

"Thanks."

As they waited for the water to boil, Roser sat down and looked at her friend.

"You look horrible."

"Worse than horrible. Why didn't you warn me?"

"About what?"

"About the size of this guy's 'instrument.'"

"What do you mean? I told you and you said I was exaggerating."

"For God's sake, Roser. Something like that is serious. You should have tried to convince me. It sounded like you were joking."

"I told you that the thing this kid has between his legs is terrible!"

The coffee was ready. Roser got up to serve a cup for herself and Montse.

"But I see that despite all that, you came back for more."

Montse smiled.

"I couldn't help myself. It's the most terrible prick I've ever seen, but I can also assure you it's the most terrific."

"You don't need to tell me. I was the first to feel it. The problem is that if we end up every morning feeling like shit, unable to get up, like you're feeling now... I'm still feeling the pain."

"We'll find a way. It's just that we're not used to this. As soon as we get the hang of it, it'll all run smoothly. Anyway, that's what I hope. This is a big win for us," Montse admitted.

"Whatever. But what are you going to do about today? Your dad is the president of your company, and he's going to find out you haven't been at work because you're sick. He'll tell your mom and she'll come running, with your aunts who live in the building, to say nothing of the cleaning lady who's coming later today."

"Truth is I didn't expect all this today, but I'll figure it out. I'll keep my family out of it by assuring them it's nothing serious. As for the cleaning lady, I'll just leave a note here on the table like always with what I owe her. I'll tell her I'm in the bedroom and not to bother me, that I'll take care of it another day, and I'll make sure to order her not to open the door for anyone as long as I'm here."

She laid out the details, then Roser left for work. Montse wrote the message for the maid. She grabbed two liters of milk, fruit, and cold cuts and went back into the bedroom. Bambara Keita washed himself and ate breakfast right there in the bedroom. When the maid came she stayed for three hours, then there was silence—she had left.

All day Montse had been receiving phone calls from her family asking about her health. She calmed their concerns. But by four they were already knocking. She stood up with difficulty and managed to get to the door. She looked through the peephole. It was one of her aunts. Of course. She tried not to be nervous. She opened the door only halfway and tried to block the other half from sight.

"Hello, Aunt Inés."

"Your father called to tell me you weren't feeling well."

Aunt Inés was about seventy-five. She was thin with golden hair.

"Papa gets worried for nothing. I told him it's just a little discomfort."

"But you're not looking good, like you're in pain."

"Just a little muscle pain. Maybe I'm coming down with something, but don't worry, Auntie. I'm fine."

The elderly woman seemed satisfied with the explanation.

"Don't you want me to make you something to eat, or anything?"

Montse knew she had to be calm not to worry anyone. This was all new to her. The family was not used to seeing her skip work because she was sick.

"I don't need anything, auntie. Don't worry. Roser came by, she made something to eat and we had lunch together. I just need some rest. Tomorrow I'll feel better."

Aunt Inés seemed convinced.

"As you wish. But if you need anything, call me. I'll be home."

"Fine, auntie, I will. Don't worry."

The old woman left. Montse closed the door and leaned her back against it. She let out a sigh of relief and went back to bed. They had made love again as soon as the cleaning lady had left. Bambara Keita, with no recourse but to obey, did not know what to do. Having to be captive in bed was tiring him, but he could not complain.

"Tonight we'll go out, get some fresh air. We need it," Montse suggested, noticing that her lover-employee was nervous. "But we'll wait till it's late."

Montse meant that they'd go out when there were no neighbors in sight. All day she had received calls from her parents, worried about her health. The same with the aunts who lived upstairs, as well as her cousin, a lawyer whose office was in the same building. She could not have left the phone off the hook, that would have been worse. They would think there was something wrong, and they would come by in person.

Around ten thirty, they got ready. She was still having difficulty walking. She went out into the hallway first, to make sure no one was around. She pressed the button for the elevator, and when it arrived she signaled for the African to come along. He obeyed, gently shutting the door behind him. They went down to the parking lot and got into Montse's car, always mindful of who might be around. The windows of the car were tinted so that it was difficult to tell who was inside.

She sighed deeply when she left the apartment building. She drove to the Olympic Port where her office was, but she did not tell her companion where she worked. She thought about telling him, but then she thought she shouldn't. You can never tell. They did not go into the port area. She had dinner there frequently, and she did not want to find any of her friends. It was risky. She drove by the walkway along the beach.

"That statue we're going by is Christopher Columbus, one of the greatest men in the history of humanity. He discovered America and brought enlightenment to that part of the world," she said, playing the role of guide and schoolteacher at once.

The African had already seen that statue because it was very close to the beginning of La Rambla, the most beautiful street in Barcelona. If Bambara Keita had visited other cities in Europe or throughout the world, he would have affirmed that without a doubt, La Rambla was the most spectacular. But at this point he was satisfied to conclude that it was pretty and that he liked it a lot. Sometimes he strolled up and down that boulevard without hurry, lost among the many kinds of people who walked along it.

He leaned over toward the windshield to get a better view of the statue.

"Do you know who Columbus was?" he heard Montse ask as he gazed at the statue.

"Oh, yes, I learn in school. He arrive in America."

Bambara Keita spoke no more. He had said "arrive," not "discover." He was a Black African. That is to say, an ex-colonized man. And like so many colonized people, he also rebelled against the expression "discover," which whites like to use when they refer to Africa or America. Both continents already had people living there when the adventurers found them. They did not fall from the sky the moment the new arrivals got there. The African thought that any expression other than "conquest" was more realistic. But of course this is something they would only talk about among themselves! Who were they to contradict the victors of history?

For his part, he was in no mood to teach his boss a lesson. He was thankful he did not have to explain his use of the word "arrive" instead of "discover." Hearing the word "conquest" in reference to Columbus would have made him articulate his most intimate thoughts. Because thinking about the dire situation of his native Africa, he might have said to his benevolent boss-lady that the so-called "discoverers," like Columbus, had brought Africa much more harm than benevolence.

Luckily Montse did not delve into the issue. They passed the statue of the great discoverer at the intersection between Ramblas and the Paseo Marítimo. Further ahead they turned right on the way up toward Montjuïc Mountain.

"Have you been to the Olympic Stadium?"

The African shook his head.

"It's right here."

The African contemplated the gigantic architectural work as Montse drove by slowly. What she was looking for was a dark spot where they could get out of the car and get some fresh air. But on the way up to Montjuïc, with all its oxygen-producing plant life, she couldn't find a secluded place. They went toward the Plaza de España. Then she came up with an idea: They would go to Tibidabo.

"Do you like Barcelona at night?" she asked.

The African, somewhat distracted thinking of the recent changes in his life, turned his attention to Montse.

"What?"

"I just asked if you like Barcelona at night."

"Oh yes. Very nice."

Yes, it's true. Barcelona is as beautiful by night as it is by day. But it was not clear that Bambara Keita could contemplate the beauty of the metropolis, his serendipitous new residence. He, like so many others, had ended up in Barcelona haphazardly. After a year and two months of being jailed at the Melilla Detention Camp, one morning the authorities grabbed a few of them and brought them by plane to Barcelona. When the plane landed it took them to a discreetly hidden place at the airport. Their feet did not even touch the ground. From the plane they were taken directly to a police truck, then to a station. And three hours later the authorities gave each one of them a sandwich and a drink.

"There you go, you're free," the one who seemed to be in charge told the captives.

That order needed no repetition. The freed ones scattered and found themselves on a great avenue. They did not know exactly where they were, but they knew at least that they were in Barcelona, because the authorities told them so. From that moment on, each one began fending for themselves. Bambara Keita was able to arrive at the Plaza de Cataluña with some of his companions. This was the place that ended up being almost a permanent home, where he depended on the kindness of others or the Red Cross. It was true that he had been in Barcelona for some time, but he did not know the city well. He would not even be able to recognize the police station, or the street where he found himself on his first day of liberty. He often walked around in the center of the city, mainly La Rambla. He had gone to some places on the outskirts of town, but he would always come back to the same place. One time he even managed to leave Barcelona. That was when an Arab friend had convinced him to go and look for work in Lleida, a city in the interior.

The work would consist of harvesting fruit. A friend who shared space with him in the Plaza de Cataluña told him there was much work there. They rounded up as much money as they could to pay for train tickets. There were five of them.

The harvest that season was abundant, so lots of work was needed for picking. But the government wanted to curtail under-the-table work. The result was to regulate hiring practices and give contracts to Central Europeans.

With government inspectors watching over the harvest work, the growers did not hire Africans who were working illegally. Bambara Keita and his friends went looking for work from field to field but with no luck. He was hungry. For three weeks all he ate was hard bread and fruit he had stolen during the night. They slept in abandoned shelters in the fields. He went back to Barcelona with his Arab friend, taking advantage of another friend who was driving there in his beaten-up old car. The other three decided to try to find work elsewhere.

Bambara Keita returned to the Plaza de Cataluña, always hoping for an opportunity. He didn't know what he might find, but he had faith in God and surely he would not be abandoned. Moreover, he didn't have time to think about anything. He did not want to. If he thought about it too much he would probably wind up regretting the day he decided to leave his town. Remorse was not an option. He could not return. He would never find enough money or resources to do so. The only thing he could do was hope, and that's what he did. But riding in Montse's car, he was having doubts. He couldn't believe that, at last, it seemed like a major opportunity had arrived.

The car was ascending a steep hill, winding around curves.

"You're very quiet, what are you thinking about?"

Montse wanted to distract him from the curves.

"No thinking."

In a way he was telling the truth. Thinking of his stay in Barcelona was the same as thinking of nothing. At the same time, he could not allow Montse to participate in his own doubts. Surely he had tasted honey, but would it last?

They were on Vallvidrera Road, in an elevated section of Barcelona where rich people lived. Montse stopped at a place that was quite dark. Further ahead there were a few cars parked with passengers inside.

"They are couples," she pointed to the cars.

"Couples?"

"Men and women doing what you and I do in bed."

She spoke this last phrase in his ear. The African laughed.

"Don't they have places to live?"

"Some do, some don't. Many of them come here because they have to hide."

"Like you, me?"

His question surprised the Catalan woman. We seldom accept that we might do exactly what we accuse others of doing.

"Well, yes, but it's not the same. Some are hiding because they are married to other people, homosexuals..."

But Montse could not explain to herself why she needed to hide the Black man, since they were both single, and therefore free.

"Oh, so in car they—"

"In the car or in whatever place they can enjoy themselves."

"People strange here, no?"

"Like everywhere, my sweet friend. Let's just take in the scenery."

They got out of the car, but they did not go far. Montse leaned on him with her back to the car.

In front of them they could see almost all of Barcelona's lights. The tall building where she worked stood out from among the others. They could see the port as well, the moored boats and their silhouettes.

From this high perspective Bambara Keita contemplated Barcelona at night for the first time. There was the city. He was now on top of it, looking down, next to a rich woman with a luxurious car. The city stood majestically before them. From a closer distance he thought about another dimension of the rich capital: its misery, a reality hidden by both the city and its citizens. The view erased their doubts, their exhaustion, and their nostalgia, if only momentarily. All these little miseries were not enough to make him unwilling to accept the benefits of this great city of white people.

When they went back to Montse's place, she took the same precautions as before. She could not breathe a sigh of relief until she closed the door. They went to bed. They did not make love. Montse, in spite of herself, did not act on her urge. She wanted to be intact the next day. She was certain her parents would visit if she stayed in bed again. She had still not prepared them with the story that she had found a Black butler for her house.

She got up at five thirty, waking Bambara Keita. Before they left the apartment, they again took the same precautions. Around six thirty she dropped the African off at the Plaza de Cataluña.

"Don't forget our plan," she told him as he got out of the car.

"No forget."

Montse started the car and left.

CHAPTER 7

ITH HIS BAG IN HIS hand, Bambara Keita went back to his old residence. He met up with two of his friends. They were just getting up from where they had spent the night.

"Hey kid, you've been gone for two days," one of his friends said in French as he approached him.

"That's the way things go in the country of the whites," he answered with a sly and proud smile.

His disposition and his new clothes made the others suspect that his luck had changed. Their suspicions were confirmed when he later invited them to have breakfast at a nearby café. When they saw him take out a wad of bills to pay for the meal, they couldn't believe it. Their suspicions turned into admiration.

"You surprise us," one of them said.

"Ah, yes, I'm telling you this is white people's business," he murmured proudly taking note of their envy.

He gave them a little money.

"Have a little of this, my friends."

The others thanked him. Hope sprang up: if their friend's luck had changed, it could also happen for them. They did not know exactly what Bambara Keita had done in two days to look so good and have all that money. But they didn't care. They didn't ask any more questions. "*Ce sont les affaires des blancs…*" he had said. It was the truth. Only in a country of whites could someone as miserable as their friend—someone who just two days ago was sleeping outside, exposed to the elements—see his luck change so drastically.

They parted ways with a sweet taste in their mouths. Bambara Keita, following Montse's instructions, went looking for a place to live. He found one on a street perpendicular to Las Ramblas. He paid for five days in advance. Then he bought a cell phone, again just as his lover-boss had asked him. When he acquired the phone he went to Western Union to send money to his family. It was the first time he had done so since he left them. During those difficult years of trying to reach the white people's country, he had not gotten in touch with his family. In many ways, he was in exile—he had been forced to leave his land because he could not find work. But at the same time, his exile was voluntary because he had left of his own volition. He had thought about this for a long time after abandoning his land.

It was after his fight with an Arab companion who was also interned in the reception camp in Melilla. The Arab had taken his ballpoint pen without his knowledge, so he went looking for it. A friend from Senegal told him that the Arab had what he was looking for. Bambara Keita tried to get it back. The North African denied having it, but he insisted. With the repeated denials, the discussion turned into a heated argument.

Between insults and curses, the Arab blurted out, "A dirty nigger like you who had to abandon his country cause he was starving!"

Bambara Keita could not allow the insult to go unanswered.

"Okay, so I left my country because I was hungry—and you? What are you doing here in jail far from your home, just like the rest of us?"

The Arab was not intimidated.

"I'm in my country. I'm in my land. Melilla, Morocco; don't you get it?" But Bambara Keita had an answer.

"You don't even believe that. If Melilla is Moroccan and you call it your homeland, what are you doing here locked up like the rest of us, under the control of those Spanish brutes?" he asked without hesitation, then added, "For your information, I didn't leave my country because I was hungry, like I'm sure you did. I left because I wanted to, because I'm young, I wanted to see the world." They had their fists raised to fight, but the guards separated them.

There were frequent fights in that camp. Mutual scorn between rivals was also common. It was there that he learned about the pain of those who leave their land because of misery and hunger. The detainees often accused each other of this. While they were all suffering under the same conditions, some thought it was their right to let the others know how despicable they were. It was also there that Bambara Keita began to believe that he had left of his own free will to seek adventure. Later he would use the expression "looking for life." But he reserved these words for whites only, the real ones, those they call the "Westerners."

At midday he got a bite to eat at a little restaurant close to his new residence. Now he was able to sit down at a table and wait for the waiter or waitress to hand him a menu without anyone staring at him with that look of disdain he was used to. He was clean and wore a nice jacket.

When he finished eating he went to his place to lie down. He slept deeply. His body needed that rest, and when he got it, he was grateful.

Montse told him that as soon as he got the cell phone he should call her. Otherwise they would meet at ten at night on the corner of the Plaza de Cataluña. He didn't call because he was not awake until the agreed-upon time. So he washed rapidly and ran off to the designated meeting place.

That was how things went for the two following days. Montse would leave early to walk Bambara Keita out of her building, she'd go to work, and in the afternoon they would meet again. It was midday Wednesday when Roser called Montse at her office.

"Montse, I can't take it anymore. Please let me have him tomorrow through Sunday?"

"I was the one who proposed we share him for three days apiece, but you didn't like that arrangement. You wanted a whole week."

"I know, it's just that I'm dying to make love with that savage."

"For God's sake, Roser, don't call him that."

"It's not offensive, it's affectionate. Okay, I won't say it again. So let me have him tomorrow. I accept your three-days-each proposal."

"Okay," Montse gave in despite her preference. "Tell him to wait for me in front of my door, on the corner, around nine. I'll pick him up."

Roser thought about it.

"I'm not sure about that, Montse. It's not safe. A Black man hanging around that area and at that time, especially in a neighborhood like yours where there are no immigrants like him. I think a neighbor might notice. You know how suspicious people can be in that area."

"You might be right. I didn't think of that. So what should we do?"

"I don't know. Maybe you can do what I do: meet him on a corner of Plaza de Cataluña and take him home with you."

"I don't know if that will work, Montse." And before the other native could reply, she added, "Then there's the problem of my car."

"What's wrong with your car?"

"It's not like yours. It doesn't have tinted windows. We don't want anyone to know who's inside."

Montse thought about it.

"Okay, so I'll take him to your door and you can both get in."

"Okay, that's fine. Thanks."

Montse was about to hang up, but then she remembered something else.

"How are you going to let him out of your house? Will you pick him up once he's on the street and bring him here?"

"I'm not going to take him out of the house. He'll just stay there until I get back."

"So you're going to shut him in your house for three days?"

"I don't think he's a thief, and if he is, there's nothing valuable he can steal without my seeing it."

"I wasn't talking about that. Three days is a long time for a person to be shut in a house."

"I know, but I don't see any other way until I get it together and tell the neighbors that I've got someone working for me in my apartment."

"I don't know."

"Don't worry, it'll be okay. I'll see what I can do."

They hung up. Roser's suggestion pleased Montse. The call had assured her that her friend had not only accepted the arrangement but also that she was a willing particpant. She laughed to herself. Why didn't this occur to them earlier? They had been wasting their time. She cursed her society, telling herself she was living in an atmosphere of repression, despite what people said. People force themselves, she thought, to hide what they really need and want.

She asked herself what her parents would think. Yes, her mother lamented that she was not married and did not have children, even though she didn't say so. But she could not imagine the torment that people endure when they don't have a sexual partner. She was sure that her mother thought she was a virgin, since she had never seen her go out with a steady boyfriend.

Poor mom! she thought. Worst of all was that social taboos kept them from talking about it. *And the both of us are getting on in years.* Fortunately things had changed a little, but that change had not affected her generation. Nonetheless, she was glad about it. Younger people were enjoying sex now. Nowadays they could talk to their parents about anything, or almost anything. Even at school there was sex education. How fortunate for them. *I'm envious!* she thought.

Montse was feeling good that day, and she wanted to spread the happiness. She would have loved to tell her family what she was feeling and why she was feeling it. She was a free spirit, and having to hide her joy was limiting her freedom. She told herself that in due time things might change for her. She wasn't content to let things remain as they were. She had taken the first step, and it was going well. She would concentrate on how to keep it going.

When it got dark she left her office. Like always, she went to see Bambara Keita at their usual meeting place. They had dinner once they got home. After dinner she told him that the arrangement had changed a bit.

"Tomorrow, you'll be with Roser, not with me."

In her voice there was something plaintive and reproachful. But there was also satisfaction. She liked her friend a great deal and she wanted her to be happy as well.

Bambara Keita didn't say anything. He had nothing to say. He was working for two bosses and he had to be where they told him to be. At the same time, the fact that the other one wanted him before it was time only confirmed that his employers were satisfied with his product.

When they went to bed, they made love. Montse, knowing that the following day she would be alone, paid special attention to her own gratification. She had become accustomed to her lover-employee's cock. Its size was still hurting her when they did it, but with time the pain was not as strong. Or perhaps the pain had become part of their sexual play: the pain of pleasure. She wanted it more and more each day.

After having sex, Bambara Keita fell asleep as usual. Montse, on the other hand, slept only for a short time. She got up to go to the kitchen for a glass of milk. When she got back to bed, she woke him up.

"Bambara Keita, make me happy again."

Her voice was soft, affectionate. It was the third time she had used that expression when she wanted him to possess her.

Bambara Keita was a little annoyed. He was sleepy. Little by little he returned to reality. His work was needed. In spite of his boss's sweet voice, he knew that she was not asking but demanding. He thought of complaining, but he kept himself from doing so. When he was in Africa, he had seen images of white peoples' countries at the movies, and he had fallen in love with them, like everyone did. With all his heart he hoped to arrive there one day to enjoy the beautiful houses and the good life. "In Europe everything is easy. Life is easy, it's not like here in our country," his African friends would say to each other.

Bambara Keita, upon his arrival to Europe, saw that all the marvelous things that he had seen on the movie screens were real, even the famous "good life." It had not been a lie. It was just that it was not easy to acquire all those things, nor to live that "good life" that some enjoyed. No one had ever told him about the difficulties. Nor did they tell him that in the white man's paradise there were some people who had to sleep outside because they had no place to go, and they had to eat what they found in the garbage, as he himself had done.

Bambara Keita didn't like to dwell on his misfortune, because he did not want to regret his decision to leave. But sometimes, when sadness invaded his thoughts, he asked himself why no one had ever warned him about how hard his life would be in the paradise of the whites. Why didn't anyone ever tell him? Why wasn't that warning given when people talked about how nice it all was? Why weren't all those ads describing elegant cars, mansions, suits—yes, why couldn't they just mention, if only for a couple of seconds, that there was also a lot of misery and injustice? Why, if even the whites talk about the bad things, can't the Blacks do it too? But he did not go far with these thoughts. He did not ask himself if he would have believed the negative side if they told him about it.

The fleeting memory of his regrets ended just as he was emerging from sleep. He should not think about that past life, at least not now. After all, he had certainly been admitted into paradise. He was beginning to acquire nice things. Montse bought him some more new clothes. He was enjoying the good life, the life of those who had been allowed to enter paradise. The only thing he had to do was work. Indeed his new job was the key that opened up the good life and all those good things.

"I've brought you some chocolate milk prepared how you like it," said Montse, extending him a steamy cup.

"Thank you," he said as he stood up.

He drank slowly as he looked at the alarm clock Montse had on her nightstand. It was three thirty. He had not slept more than forty minutes.

When he finished, Montse took the cup from his hands and put it on the table. She caressed his face.

"Are you tired, my little one?"

"Oh, no, I fine."

In fact he was tired, it's just that he did not want to acknowledge it. He was aware that his position was a delicate one. There were many competitors. They did not choose him because he was the handsomest Black man. He had no illusions about that. It was just good luck. God had something to do with it. It was his Savior who never abandoned him. In Barcelona there were thousands like him: Blacks, whites, Asians, half-white-half-Asians. But the hand of God chose him. So he had to protect his place. Jobs like this one definitely don't come along often. If it had happened earlier he certainly would not have spent almost a year wandering around the plazas and parks of Barcelona, sleeping in inclement weather.

Having come to that conclusion, he thought no more about it. He put his head directly between the woman's breasts. He searched for protection in them. Surely they were the assurance he needed that he would no longer have to endure what he had suffered. He stayed still this way for a long time with his head barely visible, feeling the warmth of her tits and smelling their perfume. Then he lifted his head and began to suck on her nipples.

"Damn Roser!" he heard her exclaim in the middle of her ecstasy. "Why couldn't she wait her turn like we planned?"

Bambara Keita did not stop to listen to Montse's monologue. He continued, tirelessly focused on the task of pleasing her.

"Keep it up, love! Keep going, don't stop! Give me what only you can give me!"

The African continued. And she continued to urge him on. She was beside herself.

"Keep going stronger! Stronger! Don't stop! Bite me a little!"

The man obeyed and went right to his task. He had never done that before. He did it gently because he did not want to hurt her.

"A little harder," she coaxed.

He bit harder.

"Yes, like that! Like that, love! Very good!"

The employee knew now that he had reached the spot she was looking for. He now knew that spot. He kept it in his mind. He kept his teeth closed, squeezing the woman's nipples in his teeth.

"Like that, good! Aaaaaaaaah!" Montse groaned. "God, I don't know what I'm going to do without you for the next few days."

As she said this, she momentarily separated herself from him and knelt down in front of him.

"Put the whole thing in my mouth!"

When he lifted his head, she saw that she was inviting him down close to the pillow. Bambara Keita went to find a condom. Her mouth was open, and so were her ass and pussy. Bambara and Montse were both silent, yet they wanted the same thing. He obeyed and satisfied her and himself. He did not have the proper number of cocks to fill her three openings at once, so he would have to rely on one. He knew that if he satisfied one of her orifices, he would satisfy them all. He slipped his hard shaft into the deepest reaches of the woman. A cry of pain filled the bedroom. And as on other occasions, Montse fell onto the bed. She liked it, but she was still not used to it. That sensation of pain was truly horrible. It had not changed since the last time. It was sharp, penetrating, paralyzing. The deep pain, the moan, and the fall onto the bed all seemed to go together, inextricable. Sometimes after a loud moan she covered her mouth, trying to keep the neighbors from hearing it. This was another gesture she was used to.

As with the other times, she lay there still until she regained her breath and strength. When she was able to, she began to slowly move her butt. That was the signal for her companion to get to work. He was motionless, although his cock was deep inside her. He knew the signal. So when he received the order, he began to move in and out as they both grew more and more excited. Once again they enjoyed the intense pleasure of each other. When they finished, Montse was disappointed they had no time to rest. They got up, dressed, and Montse dropped him back off at the Plaza de Cataluña, near his new place.

Bambara Keita went into his building. The doorman was now used to seeing him arrive at about that time. He surmised that the young man worked at some factory. He was a pleasant man, but he didn't say much, which was fortunate for Bambara Keita, who preferred not to have to answer too many difficult questions.

"So, lots of work tonight?" he asked when the African requested the key to his room.

"Oh yes, a lot. Life hard," he said, unconvincingly.

"You're young and you can take it. Not like me. My arthritis is killing me," the old man lamented as he handed him the key.

Bambara Keita took his key and went upstairs. Who would have thought that whites suffered from pain? When he was little, he thought they never died. He immediately got into bed and fell deeply asleep. He dreamed about being a teenager in his home-town. Suddenly he saw himself playing in the middle of the town with his friends. They had gone out to the forest to find fruit. This fruit was big and round. Instead of eating it they used the fruit to play games. Each boy had a stick with a sharp point like a spear.

They filed into rows. About five yards in front of them a boy stood waiting for them to get ready. He was impatient. He was kicking the ground, showing his annoyance.

"Okay, throw it," said one of the boys.

"No, not yet," dictated another one. The one in charge of throw-ing the balls continued to stomp impatiently on the ground.

"You ready yet or not? If not, I'm leaving," he warned.

"If you leave, you'll never play with us again," another one threatened. This one looked older. The others seemed to be intimidated by him. The ball-thrower's rage dissipated. He waited.

At last they were all ready. They held their sticks high above their shoulders like spears.

"Throw 'em!" The command had come from the older boy. However, according to the rules of the game, the one who was in charge of throwing the balls was the one to start the game.

"Ready?"

"Yes," they answered in unison. He reared back and threw the fruit-ball forward with all his might. The makeshift ball went flying to the right, across the line of boys who in turn threw their spears. Some missed and others hit the mark. As some of the spears reached the fruit-ball, the winners (the ones who had hit their bull's-eye), advanced to the front of the line. Bambara Keita had never managed to be among them before, but at long last he was one of the winners. After several attempts his spear was the only one to strike the fruit-ball before it stopped rolling. He jumped for joy. Those who watched from the corner of the town square were also happy. He was overjoyed that a group of girls was chanting his name. But when he went to the front of the line as the winner, someone blocked him from that privileged position. It was a giant of a man. He planted himself in front of him. No one knew who the man was or where he came from.

"I won," Bambara Keita declared.

"You haven't won anything. Don't move," warned the giant.

Bambara Keita barely reached his knee. He could not see the man's face. Once he realized that he was directly in front of the giant, everyone else disappeared.

He wanted to cry out, but just at that moment he woke from his nightmare. When he recovered from the fright and realized where he was, he shouted, "Thank goodness!"

He didn't know why he always dreamed about life in his village. He had lived in other places, in other towns, but the images in his dreams were from his childhood village. What he would like now would be to dream that he was going into his village in a luxurious car, with everyone applauding and admiring him. He had always wanted that, but now he wanted it even more. He told himself that this dream would come true.

He got dressed, ready to go out. No one was at his building's door. He rang for the concierge and waited. The old receptionist appeared, dragging his feet.

"You leaving now, Darkie?" the receptionist asked affectionately.

"Yes I pay now for days here."

Bambara Keita was not aware of this man's function in the house. He didn't know if he was an employee, the owner, or a friend of the owner's. In spite of the good relationship he'd established in the few days he'd stayed in the building, he never asked. He avoided answering questions directly, and he avoided asking them.

"Oh, yes leaving now," he answered. "I have vacation in Lleida; after, I come back here."

He was lying. He mentioned the only city he was aware of nearby, the only one he could describe if anyone asked him about it. He had been there looking for work. He didn't know much about it, except for the canal that traversed that Catalan city.

"How many days you going to pay for?"

After paying his rent, he went out onto the street. Montse had told him not to leave Roser's place for the three days they had agreed on. When he was alone he'd decided not to say he would be away at work. It wasn't to his liking. He preferred to tell the old man he would be away a few days on vacation. The doorman saw him leave for work at night, and it was normal for him to think that Bambara Keita's boss, no matter how much of a monster he might be, would give him a few days off. The affable old doorman was satisfied with the story.

CHAPTER 8

EVER PUNCTUAL, MONTSE MET BAMBARA Keita at the time they had agreed on. She drove him to Roser's place, where she could see her friend waving from across the street. Montse told Bambara Keita that it was ok to get out of the car. As he obeyed her orders, she looked around to make sure that no one had seen their operation.

Bambara Keita went toward Roser. She walked ahead of him. When she got to her door she looked in both directions. When she saw that no one she knew was around, she gestured for the African to come along. She pressed the button for the elevator, but the light indicated they had to wait for the elevator as it descended from the top floor. Roser was nervous. She was afraid she would run into a neighbor.

Just as the elevator was about to arrive, the door to the street opened. Roser mumbled something that the African couldn't understand. But he thought she was cursing her bad luck. He too was annoyed by the neighbor's appearance.

The man closed the door and approached the elevator. He was middle-aged, and he wore a nice suit.

"Good evening, Roser."

"Good evening, Andrés," she replied.

The man opened the elevator door to allow the woman to enter. Bambara Keita remained at a safe distance.

"Come along, Bambara Keita, your boss is waiting for you" she said, inviting him to step into the elevator.

"He's working for a friend of mine," she told Andrés. "He's coming to fetch something for her, and I need to have him do some things for me too," she explained nonchalantly.

"Ah," said the neighbor without giving it another thought.

He didn't even look at the African. Bambara Keita examined the man's shoes because his head was kept lowered to the floor. He could see that the man was well-to-do—an important person he surmised.

Roser and her lover-employee got out on the fourth floor.

"See you later, Andrés."

"See you," he responded as the elevator doors shut.

Roser opened the door to her apartment, and once they were both safely inside she closed it behind them. As she leaned on the door to rest a bit, she closed her eyes. When she opened them Bambara Keita was looking at her.

"What a scare, but you were great. That's just the way I want you to behave."

He nodded in agreement.

Every little cloud has a silver lining, she said to herself. "At least this has allowed me to let people know that you work for me."

Bambara Keita didn't say anything. When Roser had recuperated from the close call, she made a formal gesture inviting him into the apartment.

"You know the place, Bambara Keita."

Indeed he did. He recalled it immediately. He had entered Roser's place—overflowing with character just like the ashtrays all over the house. Montse was the neat one and Roser just the opposite. He felt a little sad now, comparing the two. But that's all he could do—compare. He was in no position to choose one or the other.

His grandfather had told him the story of the rat and the cat. The two of them were good friends at first. They were always together. But one day they went hunting and trapped an animal they both liked to eat, particularly its entrails.

"Let's eat the meat now, and leave the guts in the sun for later. It'll be tasty that way," the rat proposed.

The cat did not object. The rat was a loyal and reliable friend. They placed the animal's insides behind their houses to dry. But as the cat waited for the guts to dry, the rat cut off a little piece for himself and brought it to his house for his family to eat.

"It's probably dry by now, right?" the cat asked.

"I think in a couple of days it'll be just right," the rat assured. And the cat believed him.

But when the cat arrived at the rat's house to enjoy what they had prepared, he found no one home. The door was locked. He knocked several times but no one answered.

"Maybe I'm early." So he went to the place where the guts had been drying. Absolutely nothing was there.

The cat realized the rat had deceived him.

"When I find him, I'll kill him!" He went looking for him everywhere.

One day, as the cat looked around for the rat, he saw its head emerge from a hole in the earth. He tried to grab him but the hole was too narrow.

"I'll kill you when I catch you!" he swore. And from that moment the rat lived hidden inside its hole.

Bambara Keita's grandfather concluded: "That's why rats are always hiding. Every now and then, when no one is looking, he comes out to look for food, and that's how he lives."

The moral of this story helped Bambara Keita deal with his hiding place in Roser's house. This story would not have come back to him if the memory of Montse's posh apartment were not so vivid to him. He did not leave Roser's apartment, as she had directed him.

When she went to work, he stayed at home. He watched TV but with the sound off. Roser told him to use headphones. His presence in her apartment must remain completely unknown to anyone. He could not even play music. But even if his patron had allowed it, he would not have made any noise. The music she listened to was not at all to his liking. It had no cadence, no rhythm. Since reading was not his strong suit, he didn't pick up any books or magazines. Besides, all the books Roser had on her shelves were in Spanish, a few in German. So he opted to watch TV. Lying down on the couch with the remote in his hand, he surfed from channel to channel.

Bambara Keita grew tired of listening to the whites' trivial gossip: this one was sleeping with that one, Joe X was cheating on his wife or his girlfriend. Or Little Miss Fancy said that a lady claimed publicly that she had slept with a famous man.

The African was becoming more familiar with the white man's world. Even despite his lack of education, he could not stop asking himself why they were all so infantile, considering they had conquered so much of the world throughout history. At least they seemed that way: they just did not act like adults. How could a person's intimate relations be exposed in a public conversation for the benefit of millions of people?

He understood the precautions taken by his two bosses. A tiny misstep might come to the attention of the entire country, because the television networks reached so many eyes and ears.

"Really, whites are truly crazy," he exclaimed when he saw something he found utterly outrageous.

In any case, no matter how the whites behaved, it was not his problem. If the lords of earthly paradise acted that way, he had nothing to say. Nonetheless, all those vulgarities and banalities seemed to make that paradise more attractive every day. He became very familiar with the gossip programs on every channel, without exception. Some people called them soap operas and others "junk TV." "Junk TV" was the term he found most appropriate. But he had nothing else to do but watch it. There was not much else interesting on TV. Every once in awhile there was an action movie. But most of those were on at night. And at night he had to work.

Thus, no matter how long he slept, at the end of the day he always had time to watch TV. Sometimes he fell asleep with his headphones on. At least he was able to rest. Like anyone who works at night, he needed to sleep by day to keep up his strength.

Every now and then Montse called to find out how he was doing. The other one also called but not with as much tenderness. Every time he heard Roser's voice, he immediately wished to see Montse. She gave him a great sense of security.

Three days passed. On Sunday night, Montse came to pick him up. While they were having dinner in Roser's apartment, Montse said, "Bambara Keita, we want to tell you something." She paused. "We've been together for a week, and we want our relationship to last. Do you understand?"

"Oh, yes. Last long time! I very happy."

"Well, we are happy that you're pleased with the arrangement," Montse continued. "So, now that we all trust each other, Roser and I have decided you should have an HIV test, just so we can all be sure. You never know."

After she had let this out, she felt relieved. She'd always asked herself why the mention of sexually transmitted diseases created so much apprehension. After all, sickness is sickness. At least that's what she thought. They were like any other illness—once they appeared, they damaged the lives of everyone who suffered from it, just like cancer or anything else.

"You know that your condom can come off when you make love, and that's dangerous," added Roser.

"Oh, yes, no problem! I no have AIDS because see doctor. They make test, they see all. They say no problem."

"Yes, but we need you to have updated tests, then you show us the results. It's just so we can be sure."

As always, Montse used a voice that soothed the African and made him trust her.

"Okay, no problem. I go tomorrow."

"Do you know where to go?"

"Oh, yes! Ramblas, near Drassanes. Hospital, many immigrants. They good to immigrants. Doctors, nurses, very nice. Immigrants go there, they like. They call it 'Doctor Bada's Center.'"

The natives looked at each other. That was completely new information to them. They had no idea.

"Fine, then. Tomorrow you'll get tested," affirmed Roser.

Bambara Keita was silent for a moment. He didn't look at either of them. The natives noticed something strange on his face. They looked at each other, wondering why.

"Did you hear what I said, Bambara Keita?" Roser asked with an air of authority. Montse noticed Roser's concern, so with her eyes she asked Roser to remain calm.

"Yes, I hear. But when test come I still use condom, because I no want disease," said the African with a tone of certainty, although he was a bit embarrassed to say it.

"What?"

"Are you saying...?"

The two women were astonished at the suggestion. But the African remained calm. He remembered what his grandfather used to tell him: "Son, the most important thing in life is your health." They had gone to a brook, and while his grandfather was bathing, the boy disappeared behind some rocks. He did not want to see his granddad naked, so he played alone, jumping from rock to rock. But at one point he fell. His cry made his grandfather jump out of the water. He went directly over to his grandson, covering himself with a little towel that was old and dirty. The towel was not as old as his grandfather, but it was certainly old, very old.

"What happened to you?" he asked.

"I fell down."

Bambara Keita told the women the story. The old man had leaned down next to him, covering himself with the little towel. He did all he could to keep his grandson from seeing his private parts, because it could bring him bad luck for his entire life. Despite his concern for his grandson, he was acutely aware of the possible bad luck. His life was ending, while his grandson's was just beginning. He was now on the path toward his ancestors, but the boy would remain among the living, thereby perpetuating his existence and the ancestors' too. The boy was suffering from an injured toe. His grandfather lifted him up. When he was dressed, he helped him wash himself in the brook, but without allowing the injured foot to enter the water. Then he looked around for a special herb. He found it, crushed it, and rubbed it on the wound.

On the way back home, his grandfather told him that his health was his most important asset, "You should always know how to take care of yourself."

"Grandfather, is health more important than airplanes, cars, and lots of money?" he had asked, trying to distract the old man from his worry.

"Health is more important than anything in life," his grandfather said again. "I bet if you broke your leg you wouldn't be able to walk for a long time. Isn't that right?" the old man asked.

"Yes, you're right."

"Well, if you weren't able to walk, you couldn't have a car," the grandfather concluded.

Bambara Keita always had his grandfather's words in mind. But at this moment he found himself in a dilemma: he had to find the balance between his health and the considerable money that his bosses were paying him. His grandfather had told him that health always comes first and that he must never doubt it. So he made his request known.

"I go for tests, I sure about me, but not sure about you."

Roser opened her eyes wide, not believing what she was hearing.

"How can you think that about us, Bambara Keita?" Montse asked without losing her composure.

"Oh, yes! My father say when person points finger at you and say you bad, you know his three other fingers point to himself and say he three times badder. And fifth finger points to God."

Bambara Keita accompanied his father's saying with a gesture. He pointed to Roser with his index finger, while his three other fingers pointed back at him, and his thumb pointed up toward heaven. Even though the African said his father was the one who told this story, he knew for sure it had been his grandfather who told his father.

The two women were speechless.

"What do you mean by that?" asked Roser.

Bambara Keita knew he was taking a risk, and that he didn't have much hope of keeping his job. It pained him, but his grandfather told him never to question a decision in favor of his health. He had already decided. He had opted for his health. He said, "Oh, yes! You say I sick with your finger, but your three fingers say..." Bambara Keita hesitated, then added, "In my country I teach young about AIDS, we teach never trust anyone!"

Roser could not take any more. She got up and went to the kitchen, and Montse followed.

"As much as I need a good cock, I will not take this from anyone, much less from a full-of-shit African !"

"Calm down, Roser. It's not such a big deal."

"Not a big deal, you say? This ignoramus wants to teach us something?"

"Lower your voice, please. Someone might hear us."

"Let them hear us, I don't care! I will not allow a worthless, piece-of-dung African to humiliate me. As far as I'm concerned, he's done. I can't stand this."

"Don't take it that way, Roser," begged Montse. "These people might be poor, but they have their dignity. It looks like we offended him that we didn't trust him."

"We should be offended too! We pay him and he should do what he's told."

"And he does, Roser. But we don't pay him to get sick and die."

"What are you talking about?"

"I'm just saying we could be sick, too, and we could spread it to him."

"You think you and me could have it?"

"No, but who knows? You heard what he said. They taught him he should not trust anyone. So if we look at it from another angle, maybe this can be good for us, too. If he brings us back a negative test result, we can be sure he's a responsible person who knows how to take precautions, and that's good for us."

"His proverbs and stories are driving me crazy. They seem like they're designed to insult people."

"Maybe that's just the way he talks."

"I always thought that primitive people like him were more noble, at least when they spoke. But that guy's tongue is a deadly weapon." Roser thought for a moment. "So what should we do?"

"Well, let's just take the test. What difference will it make? There are clinics all over the place, private and discreet. Everything is perfectly okay."

Roser was not convinced. Everything would go much better if that Black man would just shut his mouth, and not just his mouth but his father's and grandfather's too. She couldn't decide which of the three was most venomous. She thought for a moment, and then gave in reluctantly.

"Don't you love to have his cock in you?"

Roser was still not in a good mood. Montse was trying to get her out of it, but it wasn't working.

Roser shrugged her shoulders. Bambara Keita's sayings had angered her. She didn't know why, but she desired him as much as she hated him. She would love to just make him shut up and make love to her. The more he kept quiet and stopped uttering any of those damn proverbs, the better.

They went back to the dining room. The African was sitting down with the same expression as before. He had no idea what they had decided. But for the first time in many days, he felt at ease. He knew they were going to fire him, but he didn't care. He was going to lose a job that paid him lots of money because he chose to follow the wise advice of his grandfather. It was that thought that made him feel he had done the right thing.

"Alright, Bambara Keita, we'll do what you suggested. We'll all get tested for AIDS," announced Montse. The African did not react. Roser looked at him suspiciously. "Did you hear that, Bambara Keita? Aren't you happy?" asked Montse.

Roser didn't understand why Montse was being so solicitous. For God's sake, he was just an African who was getting a good deal! If it was up to her, they would have thrown him out onto the street, right then.

"Oh, yes. I happy. I say thank you. My father say—"

That was the last straw for Roser. She did not let him finish.

"Enough! No more about your father, or your grandfather!"

Her shouting alarmed both the African and her friend.

"Roser, please calm down."

Roser realized she was out of control. She was ashamed of her own reaction. "I'm sorry."

Montse, as always, wanted to look on the positive side. "Surely Bambara Keita could tell us a nice proverb from his town. Isn't that right, Bambara Keita?"

The African, realizing he had upset one of his employers, tried to settle her down.

"Oh, yes! My father say me trees no talk but tree always happy when he feed a hungry person with ripe fruit."

Roser shut her eyes when the African spoke, then opened them.

"So tell us what that means," asked Montse, with a smile on her face as usual.

"I like tree. I have nothing. I poor. But I happy now, because of me you have test and you be healthy. You no sick. I happy." He was smiling.

"And on top of that, he makes jokes. Can you believe it?" asked Roser.

"I like the saying and his explanation. It's very nice. But that's enough for today," said Montse.

Montse and Bambara Keita said goodbye to Roser and left.

Two days later, the two women went separately to the clinic for testing. Bambara Keita had to wait a little longer for his results. Three days later they learned that they had tested negative.

———————

They had been at their experiment for two months, and everything was going marvelously. Bambara Keita had moved to another neighborhood not far from where he had been living before. He shared a place with some friends. Little by little his situation was becoming routine. The two women had managed to keep their family members, friends, and acquaintances—all of society, really—from learning about their activity. They had let people know that they were sharing a Black man who did odd jobs, although they never told anyone exactly what those jobs were. They didn't need to explain to many people. Bambara Keita was discretion personified, and they and were pleased.

One Saturday, when the African was at Montse's place, the two gossipy aunts who lived on the floor above hers paid her a visit. The doorman, who was very friendly to the aunts, let out that their niece had hired a Black man, so they thought they would pay her a surprise visit. Fortunately, Montse and her African were awake and dressed.

"So Montse, I hear you have a new employee," commented Aunt Inés when her niece opened the door.

"Yes, auntie. I thought I told you," she lied.

"No, I don't remember."

"Well, actually he doesn't come around every day. I share him with Roser to do some odd jobs."

"That's very good, dear; the locals are becoming more unreliable every day. They don't want to work, and then they complain that immigrants come here to take their jobs." Aunt Marta had made that comment.

Bambara Keita, having complied with the rules Montse and Roser had made for him, immediately went to the kitchen when he heard voices. The two older women sat down to chat.

"So where is he?" asked Aunt Inés.

"He's doing something for me in the kitchen. But I'll tell him to come here so you can meet him. That way if you see him around here you'll know who he is." Montse moved toward the kitchen. "Bambara Keita, can you come here for a moment?"

The African appeared. He had a screwdriver in his hand.

"This is my worker," introduced Montse. "Well, he's not exactly permanent. We've hired him to do a few things for us, like I told you."

The Black man greeted them with humility. Deception and hypocrisy were part of the oral contract he'd agreed to.

"You can go back to what you were doing, Bambara Keita," she ordered.

He obeyed and disappeared into the kitchen.

"He's very handsome," Aunt Marta said mischievously.

"And very clean," added Inés.

"Aunties, please, he's just a worker. We're just helping him out by giving him a little work. We're just being charitable."

"Sure, but that doesn't mean we can't say he's handsome. Ay, when I was young!" Aunt Marta said mischievously.

"Auntie, don't talk that way about a youngster. He's a kid—didn't you see his face?" Montse was feigning indignation.

"That's exactly what I mean. I said 'when I was young.'"

"He looks like Salvador," recalled Aunt Inés.

"Yes, he looks strong, although Salvador was a little bigger. But what a man!"

Montse knew they were talking about someone who worked for them in Cuba, but she feigned ignorance.

"Who is this Salvador?"

"The man we had in Cuba who supervised the workers," Marta informed.

"He was beautiful," added Inés.

After half an hour of comments about the physical attributes of Salvador and the African, they left. They had noticed no indiscretion. Montse and Roser always knew how to make sure nothing happened that would give their arrangement away. Except for one day when Roser came over to Montse's place.

"Do you know what your doorman told me? He said that ever since Miss Torres hired that Black guy who comes by here every now and then, she seems much happier." Roser imitated the doorman's tone.

Montse was livid. "That bastard dared to tell you that?"

"Just like that. But I didn't notice any insinuation in his voice."

"He better not have. Because if he does, I'm gonna... He doesn't know me!"

"Well, I also wanted to tell you that yesterday I saw your psychiatrist, Dr. Macarrulla. He asked about you. He said that he hasn't seen you in a long time."

"No, I'm not seeing him now. I no longer have the problems he was treating me for. I'm sleeping perfectly, no anxiety. Let him get rich with other people!" said Montse.

Bambara Keita spent most of the day sleeping. Of course. The two natives, despite the fact they were no longer twenty, had given in to their fantasies and imaginations. Their hunger for sex, repressed for many years for a variety of reasons, was being satisfied. The man had the impression that these two women had never made love before in their lives.

"Hell, with all the men I see in this city, you'd think a few would give us what we want," Montse exclaimed one day when she got home. Her exigencies were getting stronger every day. Montse was the one whose desire burned most strongly. "I'd like to take you on a trip out of the country. I'd like to go where no one knows us, to be free of everyone and everything."

Bambara Keita prayed to God for that moment not to arrive. Alone, with Montse, out of the country, free of her relatives, of anything that might inhibit her. He wasn't sure he would live to tell the story. He couldn't believe it.

God forbid! he said to himself when she told him. At that moment he was thankful for the repression that society had exerted on his boss. If it weren't for her, he would still be sleeping on park benches in Barcelona's public squares. Thanks to that repression and to these two rich women, he was able to rest.

When it was her turn to be with Bambara Keita, Montse went at it with even more fervor, seeking new positions, new experiences. She wanted him to take her in the bathtub. In the bathtub no less! It would have been a great place for sex were it not for Montse's size. Bambara Keita did all he could to keep his balance and complete his task.

He could not show any form of preference, for indeed there was competition between the two natives. It's not that either of them had implied anything like that, but he was conscious of it. He had to satisfy all their whims, and when all was said and done, it wasn't so terrible. So there he was in the bathtub, making Montse happy. After a few attempts, she managed to find a position that was more or less workable. With one leg inside the tub and the other outside it, she offered herself to her man. As usual, Bambara Keita concentrated on giving his boss maximum pleasure. And with God as his witness, he would get it done! But he had to use a lot of energy and strength.

All this reminded him of a lesson that his grandfather had taught him about kola nuts. Mercifully he had been able to find kola nuts in Barcelona, in stores that sold tropical foods. When he was a little boy he had seen his father and his grandfather chew them. One day when he had accompanied his grandfather to the village meetinghouse, he asked him why he liked to eat kola nuts.

"Because they are very good," his grandfather replied.

"Really? Can I eat them too?" the boy asked.

"Children should not eat kola, but I'll let you try it." His grandfather broke off a piece with his teeth and gave it to Bambara Keita, who put it in his mouth and started to chew.

"Puf!" He spit it out. "It's sour!" His grandfather started to laugh hard, as the child frowned at him. "You lied," he told the old man.

"I did not lie to you. I told you it was not for children, but you insisted on trying it." But in just a little time, the boy became addicted to kola nuts. His grandfather called him, had him sit down next to him, and said, "Kola is good medicine for adults. It's got a lot of energy. When you're older and you need strength, you'll see how kola gives you energy when you chew on it."

Indeed, God knows it gave him energy! He had never before chewed so many cola nuts. He no longer tasted the bitterness. And even though he didn't like the taste, he kept on eating them, because his grandfather had assured him that they gave him strength, and they did.

It was strength that he most needed at this time for this particular job. He couldn't be sure if it was the kola nuts that were giving him strength, but he ate them anyway.

One day he went to the clinic on Dressanes Street and asked the doctor if there was something to give him stamina, maybe vitamins.

"You lost your appetite? Aren't you eating well?" the doctor asked.

"I hungry and I eat much, doctor, but I tired all the time." The physician looked at him. He had bags under his eyes but he seemed to be in good health.

"Do you work a lot? Is your work difficult?"

"Yes, I work very hard. Carry heavy things." While it was a lie in the strict sense, Bambara Keita was telling the truth. Montse alone was very heavy. And that little lie might turn out to be what got him the prescription for vitamins. At least that's what he was used to in the clinics in Africa.

The doctor asked him to take a blood test, because he wanted to find out if his patient suffered from a form of anemia, although neither his eyes nor his tongue indicated it. All the tests came back normal, but the doctor, just to acquiesce, prescribed vitamins for him. Bambara Keita took them secretly. He never took them to either of his bosses' homes. He didn't want to show the least bit of weakness. As he got to know his two employers he understood that both needed his strength. He chewed his kola nuts and took the vitamins prescribed by the doctor. He could not tell which of the two remedies was helping more. And he didn't need to know. The most important thing for him was to keep those two lover-beasts happy.

And while Montse required his utmost attention to satisfy her whims, Roser was equally demanding. Roser did not want to try out all the many scenarios and positions of her friend, but she was exacting. She loved the kitchen countertop. Fondly she recalled the second day they were together, when Bambara Keita had been trying out the sex positions he'd seen in the movies. She often asked him to do it again in that same place.

But all this would be nothing unusual if both women ever got tired, if only for a little while. Bambara Keita could not figure out where they got so much energy. He never heard either one of them say, "Tonight I would rather not make love." Or when they were at it, neither of them said, "Enough, I can't." And the times he tried to shorten the lovemaking, he noted they were a little disappointed. Particularly Roser. "What happened today? Have you been with another woman? Did you go see a couple of your girlfriends in your neighborhood?"

Bambara Keita had done everything he could to coax his bosses, if only once, into saying that they were tired, or at least satisfied. He yearned for one of them to tell him to please stop. But that never happened. The size of his instrument no longer dissuaded them. Sometimes he would thrust hard to hurt them, but nothing.

It looked like they were in pain, at least that was how it seemed. But it was apparent that the pain enhanced their pleasure. On these occasions it seemed to him that they were experiencing more pleasure than pain. Maybe they even needed the pain to achieve maximum pleasure.

The African, who had never had a sexual experience with a white women except once in his neighborhood, asked himself if white women ever became tired of sex. Or if the sex itself ever exhausted them, which is about the same thing. On one occasion he'd heard some of his friends talking about how white women really knew how to make love, not like Black women, who immediately cry out, "Okay, finish already!" One of his friends disagreed—he said that they weren't all the same. Some white women also tired easily, and some Black women could go without stopping.

Bambara Keita likened this second type of Black woman to the ones he was with at the moment. They didn't get tired and they never got enough. They always wanted more and more. He remembered the woman who lived with him while he was working in the post office back in his country. Her name was Josephine. He smiled thinking about her, and his heart was delivered, if only for a moment, from the anguish he was feeling. When they made love after about forty or forty-five minutes, she said to him in Pidgin, "Papa, tell that assassin your little momma is tired." Indeed his cock was an assassin to her. She would say that many times, and he liked it. They got so excited that normally they reached orgasm in unison.

He longed for those moments. It was strange that in this earthly paradise he recalled those little moments and other things about his homeland with such tenderness. They were little things that had no significance, but in his exile they seemed like treasures hidden in a sunken ship. He was living in Europe, and he was enjoying not one but two white women, and, if that weren't enough, they were rich. But curiously, deep down inside, he still wasn't happy. He missed the bed he had shared with his lover! Those strolls through town, the funky smell of roasted fish and meat, pastries of wheat or corn flour, and the loud music coming from open-air stores and bars. And what could he say about the first years of his life, in the town where he was born? What would he give to return, to run barefoot, chasing after a ball made of dried banana leaves? And the evenings at dusk, listening to the old men talking in the meetinghouse. What would he give for just one day in the city where he had studied or his hometown?

In his moments of sadness, which were quite frequent these days, he remembered his native land. Until then he had never regretted having made that long journey. But now things were changing. There were days when he lamented having embarked on that adventure.

From the moment he left his country, he could not say that he had had many moments of peace, although he never lost hope. The trip was arduous, treacherous. And when at last he found his dream job it was as if that weren't enough. There were times he wanted to quit. Sometimes he'd like to tell these ladies to go to hell, especially when they insisted he satisfy their absurd whims, and even more so when they would not even acknowledge that he was not a machine but a human being like any other. But how could he make them understand? He certainly could not rebel, much less have the satisfaction of telling these women where to get off. In the neighborhood apartment he shared with other immigrants, two of his roommates worked as busboys in a restaurant. They left in the morning and didn't come back until well after midnight. And they worked almost every day. Another one worked in a shop on the outskirts of the city. He got up around four in the morning and got back in the afternoon. Another one worked in a factory. He never seemed to be in the apartment because he was always working. And among all his peers no one made as much money as he did. These two women were paying him astronomical wages

He could consider himself privileged in a society like the one he was living in, that shamelessly exploited immigrants who had abandoned their countries precisely to find a better life, indeed to find justice. This was the peace and respect for human rights that Europe preached in all corners of the world. But Europe—the West, paradise on earth, or whatever you wanted to call it—had holes, imperfections, mistakes. It was all a farce, a façade. All image. Behind the surface of things, there was reality. The only thing that mattered was winning, so that you could acquire more things. The problem was that you didn't discover all these imperfections until you were trapped inside the system, when getting off the path was impossible. You couldn't even imagine it. How could he go back to his country of origin without the riches Europe had promised? His family, friends, and acquaintances wouldn't understand, nor would they forgive his failure. The one who leaves to conquer Europe is a hero, and he will be so until the end. That is, until he got what he set out to get, or died. Many stayed in supposed paradise just waiting to die. When they came to understand how hard life in Europe really was and how impossible it was to amass that promised fortune, they concluded the only way out was belly up.

When Bambara Keita arrived at that conclusion, he said to himself that he should trudge on. Because compared to the situation of his peers, he was better off. He had been luckier than the ones who worked in the restaurant, those working with no fixed hours in factories or fields. Of course those who found work were better off than those who had to sleep on the streets in the rain and sleet, in parks and plazas, in the cold or heat, as he himself, Bambara Keita, had done not too long ago. Yes, his situation was better! But was it really? Making love several times a week to women who weren't exactly to his liking, and who had begun to disgust him. What was better? Was this a life? Life worth living?

Sometimes he told himself that it was not a good idea to ask these questions. In his bad moods he thought he had to anesthetize the part of his brain that asked those questions. He acknowledged he had acquired things: He wore nice clothes, he sent money home to his family (of course without telling them how he had gotten it, even though it wasn't that that worried him). He knew that if his family found out about his work one day, they would not denounce him or deny its viability. They wouldn't criticize his conduct. On second thought, maybe his grandfather would have, but he was dead. He would be the only one who might have said something about it. Perhaps he would have told him a story whose moral was that you can't buy happiness, or that one should enjoy daily sex with the one you truly love. And later he would definitely tell another story concluding that a life of material deprivation in a jungle town is richer than a life swimming in riches in some corner of the West where you think you're a king, when in reality you're a slave.

But old-timers like his granddad were no longer the rule among Africans. They had left this world, and with them went their good advice and the continent's real values. Few remained.

The elders of today don't think like his grandfather. They lack dignity. Those who govern, as well as those who are governed, all act as though they were beggars. He was sure that his own parents would encourage him to keep up his work. He had no doubt about that. Africa was not only going through an enormous economic crisis, it was also enduring a dramatic moral crisis.

These thoughts overwhelmed him in the solitude of his bedroom, where weariness and indignation invaded his mind. Never before had he thought about his country or his continent in this way. There the only thing a young man like him yearned for was to leave and arrive in Europe. It didn't even matter which country.

"My poor country, poor Africa. We have failed, all your children. Poor Africa!" he found himself murmuring one day.

But then he would tell himself that, after all he was in Europe, and he had to trudge on. He had to survive. And survival meant continuing his work satisfying his two bosses—his two lovers.

CHAPTER 9

ONE MONDAY AROUND MIDMORNING, ROSER called Montse at her office, but the person who answered told her she had not come to work because she wasn't feeling well. She called her at home. She didn't want to waste any time.

"When I called your office they told me you weren't feeling well."

"Yes, I couldn't go. I wasn't feeling well."

"What's wrong with you?"

"I can't tell you over the phone. If you come here, I'll tell you."

"I'll come by this afternoon after work."

"Fine." They both hung up.

Roser appeared at Montse's place at the agreed time and knocked on the door. When Roser entered Montse quickly shut the door. She walked with difficulty toward the sofa and plunged into it facedown. She looked ridiculous.

"What happened to you?" Roser asked anxiously.

"That animal broke my butt!"

"What?"

"Bambara Keita has wrecked my ass, I'm telling you."

"But how? Don't tell me he raped you!"

"No, he didn't rape me. I asked for it, but he turned my behind into a piece of junk."

Roser was speechless.

"What? Did you ask that savage to let you have it in the behind?"

"That's it," she replied. "He tried to move but he cried, 'Ay, that hurts.'"

"I'm gonna have a word with that Black guy."

"It's not his fault. I asked for it. He didn't even want to. He said he had never done it before. But I told him I'd like to try."

"For God's sake, Montse, you're crazy. You could do that kind of thing with other men, but not with Bambara Keita. He's got a monster between his legs."

"So now my butt is suffering the consequences."

Montse tried to laugh, but all she could do was grimace.

"Don't make light of this, Montse. We might like the guy's dick, but let's be honest: it's a monster."

"I was dying to do it like that. I read a book about different positions and sexual pleasures. One part describes anal sex. So I decided to try it with him last night."

"With *him*? Try it with that animal? For God's sake, Montse, Bambara Keita is a monster, how many times do I have to tell you?"

"He's a good kid, poor little guy," said Montse.

"Sure, he's a nice guy, but I keep telling you that his prick is a monster. I don't know if I told you, but sometimes I can't even look at it. If I look at it before he enters me I think I'll probably not want to make love. It's not that I'm scared, it's more like panic. And you want to do weird things with him. Wow!"

"Who would you rather I try those things out with? He's our man. He's the perfect one."

"I would never do such a thing, not with a brute with a dick like that."

"It does hurt a lot. I think I've got a fever."

"So why don't you call the doctor?"

"And what do you propose I tell him? That a Black guy I hired to fuck me just ripped through my ass with his prick? No thank you!"

"So what are you going to do?"

"Nothing. It's not important. I just took a painkiller. I'll be fine. I can stand up now. You should have seen me this morning."

"I swear I don't understand you. Knowing what that kid has between his legs, you go and let him stick it into your rear end. That's crazy!"

"Don't tell me you don't fantasize about certain kinky things that might make you happy."

"Of course," Roser admitted. "But I hope it never occurs to me to give that barbarian my ass and let him take it. Never with him!"

"Okay—it hurt me then and it does now, but honestly, I'll tell you it's the best sexual experience I've ever had in my life," Montse said seriously. "Look, yesterday Bambara Keita prepared a great dinner for me, *fufu*, oxtail in a tomato sauce with Swiss chard. It wasn't the first time he cooked it for me."

"Yes, he made that *fufu* stuff for me too, but I didn't like it. It's too heavy," replied Roser.

"That's just why I like it. It really fills up your belly, and with a good red wine it's even better. And afterwards you really feel like making love. It's an aphrodisiac. Excellent. You can bet on it. Yesterday, after dinner, I had an irrepressible urge to make love, so I couldn't resist trying out something new."

Roser just looked at her, not knowing what to say.

"It's the best pain I've ever experienced, I swear," said Montse seeing that her friend was not saying anything. "I'm going to try it again. You should too."

"No way. You think I'm crazy?"

"It's your loss."

Roser went back to her place. Later Bambara Keita buzzed the intercom next to the building's entrance. She let him in. He was now able to come in alone, because Roser had let it be known that he was her employee. But despite his new confidence in his own comings and goings, he always entered with great humility. When he ran into someone at the door, he always bowed and greeted them politely. Roser's building didn't have a special elevator for the help. She lamented this, because that way she could avoid having the Black man run into her neighbors.

The African arrived at the door and greeted her.

"Hola!"

"What have you done to Montse?"

The tone of her voice scared him.

"I no do nothing to Montse, she fine when I go out of her house."

"You call doing what you did to her ass 'fine'?"

"Oh, yes! I no fault. I say no, she say yes."

"You should have told her no. Why didn't you just say no, when you knew you could hurt her like you did?"

"Oh, yes! I first say no. But my grandfather say you only have one life. Ancestors' life and this life, the same. This why man should always do good, what people ask him. If someone ask me do something good for him, I do it. When I go with ancestors I do same."

"Didn't you tell me that you're a Christian and that you're going to heaven?"

"Oh, yes," he said again, and assured her he would go to heaven. "But my grandfather believe he live down here with ancestors."

"So which is it?" she demanded.

"I go to heaven, and when in heaven I do like grandfather, when someone ask for something they like I say yes, I give. I no say no to person I love."

"You have an answer for everything, and it looks like it's a family thing, because your father and grandfather always have answers too," she replied, not without irony.

"My grandfather and my father very wise."

"Yes, I see that. But don't you dare do it with me that way."

"No, no. You no ask, I no do. But," he added, "if you ask I do because I love you."

"Sure, you're just a good Samaritan."

The incident passed without lasting consequence. Montse recuperated, and as she had said she would, she had anal sex again with Bambara Keita, who remained true to his beliefs. He did not deny anything to either of his two bosses. He aimed to please, and his aim was on target.

CHAPTER 10

IT WAS TUESDAY MORNING. MONTSE was in her office when her secretary received a telephone call.

"Excuse me, Ms. Torres, you have a call from the Hospital Clínico de Barcelona. He says he's Dr. Guitard."

"Dr. Guitard? I don't know who that is. I'll take it."

"Ms. Montserrat Torres?" she heard a masculine voice ask.

"Speaking."

"Excuse me for bothering you."

She sensed the man speaking to her was hesitating.

"No bother. How can I help you, doctor?"

"Señora, this is Dr. Guitard. I'm head of the Department of Pulmonology at the Hospital Clínico de Barcelona. I'm dealing with a curious case." The doctor was having a hard time getting to the point.

"Go ahead. Tell me!" Montse's curiosity had been awakened, and she grew impatient.

"I was saying, Madame, that I have a curious case. There is a Black man here who says his name is Bambara Keita."

Montse felt her heartbeat quicken. She didn't wait for the doctor to finish his sentence.

"Has something happened to him?" she asked anxiously.

"Yes and no."

"What do you mean, doctor? Please explain," begged Montse anxiously.

"It's that the young man in front of me now says his name is Bambara Keita, as I told you, and that he works for you. That's why I called."

Montse thought that as long as people thought the Black man was working for her legitimately there was no need to worry.

"Yes, I do know him, he does odd jobs for me." She wanted to keep an ace up her sleeve, just in case this had to do with some labor complication.

"We have another young man of the same race here, but he's dead. He came in under the same name, Bambara Keita, from Mali."

"What's this mess about, doctor? And what do I have to do with it?"

"Madame, it's difficult to explain this over the phone. May I ask you to come down to the hospital to identify the one who's alive? That would help us solve this riddle."

Montse thought about it. She needed to remain calm. It was not unusual for a hospital to ask someone to identify a body. The difference was that in this case they were asking her to identify a live body. That relieved her.

"Alright, doctor. I'll come by in a few minutes."

"Thank you, Señora. Ask for the Department of Pulmonology."

They hung up. Montse then told her secretary not to accept any calls for her since she was going to be out for a little while. "I'm not sure how long I'll be gone."

She went right to her car and got in. Twenty minutes later, she parked near the Hospital Clínico. When she got to the Department of Pulmonology she asked for Dr. Guitard.

"I'm Dr. Guitard. Ms. Montserrat Torres, I assume."

"Yes, that's me," announced Montse.

Dr. Guitard was about forty years old, of medium height. A prominent bald spot covered most of his head.

"Please come with me," he asked politely.

She followed him to an empty room with a table and two chairs. He invited Montse to sit down. She did, and so did he.

"As I told you over the phone, this is a strange case."

The doctor blinked. His eyes rested behind glasses with modern frames that made him look young despite his baldness.

"I don't understand," murmured Montse. She didn't know what else to say.

"Two days ago, a Black man came into the emergency room and gave the name that I told you over the phone. He was suffering from pneumonia, and unfortunately we could not cure it, despite all our efforts."

The physician's tone changed. The doctors were accustomed to seeing people die, but they were not used to failure, especially failures that ended in the death of their patients. That's what Montse was thinking when she noticed the expression on the face of the man she was talking to, and she admired him for it. She thought that for doctors one more death wouldn't be exceptional, but she was wrong in this case, and that pleased her.

"Did he die?"

"Yes, unfortunately, as I told you, he died. But later my colleagues told me that there was a problem. When the deceased's papers were being processed, his friends seemed to say the dead man's name was not Bambara Keita. That he was from Nigeria, not Mali. His passport proved it. That's when Bambara Keita, the live one, presented himself to verify his identity."

Montse was speechless. It was a mess she couldn't understand. How the hell can things like that happen? How could it be? Someone with a name dies and then it turns out that it wasn't his name, and that the one with that name is someone else. And that someone else was the Black man she knew. Of all the Black men in the city, she had to get involved with this one, Bambara Keita. This is crazy!

"May I see the one who says he's Bambara Keita?"

That was all she managed to say when she realized the doctor was staring at her. Her suggestion seemed to calm the doctor's anxiety as well. He understood that he was inconveniencing a high-class woman. He had never met her, but he intuited she was from a Barcelonan family with a pedigree. He stood up, a bit nervous, determined to figure out what this was all about once and for all. It seemed to him like something that could have appeared in a thriller novel.

"Yes, of course. Please come with me!"

Montse stood up too. He graciously moved her chair for her. They went down the stairs to the basement. Nearing the morgue she saw a group of Africans. There were six of them, and one was Bambara Keita.

"Do you know this gentleman?" asked the doctor, indicating Bambara Keita.

"Yes, that's Bambara Keita, my employee," affirmed Montse.

Bambara Keita was distraught like the rest of them. Their faces expressed their grief. He did not dare look his boss-lover in the face. Actually he never looked her in the face. Montse had asked him several times why he always looked down when he spoke to her, but the African always denied doing so. But he did. His traditional upbringing had taught him that custom from childhood, and he couldn't rid himself of the habit.

"I want you to look me in the face, because that way I can see your eyes, which, by the way, are very dark and pretty," she would tell him. He would try to do as she wished, but he wasn't always successful.

"What happened, Bambara Keita?"

"Oh, yes!" It was difficult for the African to speak.

He looked down. But at that moment he tried to look at her, and she saw evidence of tears.

"Tell me what happened," she insisted.

He pointed at the door to the morgue and told her that the dead man had been his friend, and that he had gotten ill but did not have proper documents. "I give him my passport to go to hospital. But he die."

His breaking voice was contagious. As he sighed, his friends also broke down. They all wiped tears from their eyes.

The doctor lowered his head and shook it from side to side. Montse tried not to show her emotion. She saw the other Africans crying in silence. They were all young, about the same age as the one she had hired. Something very deep touched her heart. She had never been close to an immigrant except for Bambara Keita. And until then she had never truly understood the dilemma of immigration, the difficulties, the enormity of all the problems that immigrants had to endure.

Montse seemed paralyzed by the moment. She admired the generosity of her employee.

"What can we do, doctor? I understand this is unique, even for you."

Montse wanted desperately to fix the problem and leave as soon as possible. It wasn't that she feared being associated with Bambara Keita beyond what she wanted them to know about their working relationship. She just wanted to get out of there.

The doctor tried to smile, but it was artificial: "There's always a first time. What we need to do is get in touch with the Nigerian consulate so that they can identify him. The burial is not our affair. I don't think we can do anything else."

Bambara Keita assured them he and his friends would raise the money needed to send the dead man's body back home.

"No problem, the hospital will take care of getting in touch with the consulate," the doctor told him.

It was an embarrassing situation both for Montse and for the doctor. Neither was able to express what they were feeling.

"Bambara Keita," said Montse, "you can take the day off to deal with the death of your friend."

She said goodbye to the doctor and left. As she drove, she didn't know what to think. She was worried that Bambara Keita had broken their agreement never to mention her name, but then she realized that he had had no recourse. She also thought of his endearing gesture, coming to the aid of a dying friend. She admired his solidarity. He had made his way into her heart. Too bad his generosity had ben in vain—he had been unable to save his friend's life. When she got back to her office, she called the African on her cell phone.

"It's me. How are you?"

"I fine."

Again she heard the sadness in his voice. She knew that if he said he was fine, it was because he didn't know what else to say, especially knowing that he had dragged her into the mess against her will.

"Are you still at the hospital?

He told her he and his friends were on their way out, and then he apologized.

Montse didn't allow him to finish the apology.

"Don't worry about it. Do you want me to pick you up in the same place at nine?"

"If you want."

"Sure, I'll do that. I'm sorry about your friend."

She hung up. It was her turn to be with him. She could have told him he did not have to come to her place if he wanted to be with his friends, but she didn't because she imagined how worried he must have been because of what he had done. She didn't want him to think she was going to break their agreement because of what had happened.

Next she called Roser to invite her to her place that afternoon. For the rest of the day she was distracted, she couldn't concentrate. Something was bothering her. Was it the fear she had felt when she found out that someone had associated her with the Black man? Or perhaps it was the direct knowledge that some human beings lived in such harsh conditions. No, her thoughts didn't go that deep.

She picked up her Black man at the specified time and brought him home with her, with all the usual precautions. Bambara Keita was still not allowed to come and go from her house as he pleased. Every now and then on a Saturday in the daytime he might enter and leave alone, but at night he always had to have Montse by his side, and they always used the parking lot elevator.

Bambara Keita was in the bathroom when Roser arrived at Montse's place. Montse told her what had happened that morning. Roser was livid.

"I can't believe it!" she exclaimed.

"Well, believe it."

"But why did he give them your name?"

"I don't know. I imagine because he was desperate."

"Do you realize what could have happened if someone from around here found out?"

"Nothing would have happened, Roser. The kid was prudent enough to tell them he was my employee. The worst that could have happened would have been for them to accuse me of hiring an illegal immigrant, nothing more."

"Well you're very bold, because I'm not sure I'd have gone to the hospital," Roser admitted.

"Not going there would have made things worse. It would have created suspicion. But you know, I was really moved by the generosity of those guys, the way they stuck together. The story about the mistaken identity is so bizarre, but it's so human too, anguishing. I don't know how to explain it. When we were on our way over here, he told me the dead guy had been a good friend. They traveled here together, and they helped each other when they needed it. Don't you think that's a lovely thing?"

"I don't deny it, I'm just saying that I wouldn't have dared going there. What do you want me to say? Luckily he gave them your name, not mine," she sighed.

"Roser, put it into your head that you're not doing anything illegal. What we're doing might be abnormal, but it's not illegal. We're just keeping it a secret because it's strange, not because it's illegal. We're keeping it a secret mainly because we're dealing with a Black guy. We should be aware of that. We hide him because of our reputations and because he's Black. Just admitting that will help us get out of jams like this."

"I know all this, Montse. I know! But sometimes I'm scared. I can't help it."

"Well, to relieve some of that fear I've decided I'm going to draw up a labor contract with Bambara Keita," Montse announced.

"A labor contract?"

"Yes! I'm going to enter into a legal work agreement with him. That way I'll make our situation legal."

Roser said nothing for a moment. She thought about it before asking: "Are you going to say that he..."

Montse gave a hint of a smile.

"Don't worry. I'm not going to go into the details of what he really does. Unfortunately what he does isn't even recognized by the law, much less by the population at large, even though people do it all the time. I'm going to call him a home repairman, then perhaps I can help him change his residence status with the government."

"Do you think you can make that happen?"

"You should ask if *we* can make it happen, because we're in the same boat."

"Well..."

"I think we can. I've made a few calls, and they told me it can be done."

They heard the bathroom door open.

"Don't scold him, okay? He's feeling bad right now."

"Don't worry, I won't say a thing."

Bambara Keita entered the living room and greeted Roser.

"Sorry for what happened to your friend. Montse just told me about it."

"Oh, yes, thanks."

"If you like I'll make a light dinner, and we can all eat together," Montse said as she stood up.

Roser followed her into the kitchen.

"I'm sure what happened to his friend is hurting him," commented Roser.

"I think so. People have feelings, after all. He's probably thinking it could have been him—dying far away from home, with no one close."

"But he had his friends. Didn't you say Bambara Keita was with his buddies?"

"Yes, there were six of them, I think."

Roser kept silent as she watched Montse prepare the meal.

"Did you notice if any of them looked at you in a certain way?"

"A certain way? How?"

Roser did not answer immediately. She thought about what she was about to say. "Well, I'm asking if they seemed to know, if they smiled sarcastically or something. I don't know."

"For God's sake, Roser, they were upset about the loss of their friend! You should have seen the expressions on their faces. It was sad. Bambara Keita couldn't hold back his tears when I asked him what had happened. The look on his face told me he wouldn't have even cared if I was mad at him." She paused. "For the whole day I haven't been able to think of anything else. I've never seen an expression like that. He was so dejected. Then, when I thought about it, I wondered if he regretted having come here, having suffered all that just to get here. It wasn't right that his friend had to die that way, without having realized his ambitions. Really, I was touched by it."

Roser was thinking.

"You're right. I'm being silly. I thought maybe Bambara Keita had told them about our situation, and when they saw you, they knew. I don't know."

"Don't let yourself think those bad thoughts. Up to now the kid has shown us he is discreet and responsible. We certainly can't complain. We told him not to tell anyone and it looks like he's kept the secret."

"You're right. I'm sure if he had told someone about us, you would've realized it immediately. All men are idiots like that. When a friend tells them they're sleeping with a woman, they act like clowns when they see her."

"He hasn't told them anything. I could tell he was nervous when I got there. But really what I saw in all of them, I'm telling you, was pain, lots of it."

When they finished preparing dinner, they set the table. As they were eating, Montse said to Bambara Keita, "You told me you don't have your papers in order, is that right?"

The African didn't answer instantly. He was trying to figure out the intention behind his boss' question.

"Don't worry," assured Montse. "I'm asking because we want to help you get your documents in order."

Even when the idea was her own, Montse included Roser.

"Oh, yes! I no have papers. I want have papers. I..." After a reflective pause, Bambara Keita told them that he was thinking about trying to legalize his situation. He recalled once again what his grandfather had told him: life is a continuous negotiation. He was not in the best situation in regards to his residence status, but he would not accept defeat. If he gave up it would not be a negotiation but a surrender.

"And how do you plan to go about it?" asked Roser.

Roser's question was designed to diminish Bambara Keita's plan, because the only way he could do this was through her and Montse's efforts. At the same time she was relieved, because if people saw that the Black man could move about without fear of the authorities, there would fewer suspicions.

"Oh, yes! Government is telling how to do it, and I can."

But he did not give any details. Life in Africa was so different than in Europe, but at the same time both amounted to continuous negotiation. He needed his boss-lovers, but at the same time he didn't want to let it out that he knew that if it weren't for them he'd be lost. In his native Africa, that was called politics. No one ever defined the word, which had been brought to his land by the whites. Every definition he had heard was nebulous and imprecise. Many had concluded that politics was the art of saying what you did not really believe, not always telling the truth, or telling just half of it.

It wasn't until much later that he understood what his grandfather was saying that afternoon in his town. The old man had said that life is a negotiation, which was the same as saying that life is politics. That evening they couldn't light grandfather's lamp because they were out of lamp oil. He gave his grandson a container and told him to fetch some golden oil, a substance his grandfather told him was more valuable than all the gold in the world.

"Tell the vendor to give you a hundred francs worth of oil and I'll pay her later," his grandfather said. The boy left. The woman who sold the oil lived on the other side of town. When the boy got there, he told her what his grandfather wanted. The woman was hefty, a little younger than his grandfather, although she didn't have many teeth left.

"Tell your tight-ass grandad that if there's no money, there's no oil. I'm not going to give him anything unless he pays me everything he owes."

The boy went back to his grandfather empty handed, relaying word for word what the woman had told him.

"Sit down here and wait for me. I'll be right back." The grandfather took the bottle, grabbed his long cane made from a tree branch, leaned on it, and left. Bambara Keita waited for him. He was sitting on a wooden bench. He was scared, even though there was a waxing moon and lots of stars that night. He heard the voices of other children playing at a distance from his grandfather's cabin. The nearest houses belonged to his mother and his stepmother. He was tempted to wait for his grandfather in one of those cabins, but he didn't because he knew the women would kick him out immediately—men were not allowed inside after dusk. An owl hooted from a tree at the edge of the forest, just in front of the houses along his street. He was paralyzed with fear, but he tried to endure it.

His grandfather returned after a short while.

"Here. I'll go inside for the lamp. Careful not to spill the oil." The bottle was full. Minutes later, on their way to the Meeting House, he asked his grandfather if he had paid the woman. The old man answered that he could not pay her anything, because he had no money.

"So what did you do? She told me you didn't—" His grandfather did not let him finish.

"I negotiated. Life is give-and-take, son." The boy wanted to know what that word meant.

When they arrived at the Meeting House, they sat down on bamboo mats, and his grandfather told him a story: There was an ant that had crops that were ready to harvest. One day an elephant asked the ant if he could have some of his crops to eat. The ant knew that the elephant's appetite had no limits.

"Mr. Elephant," said the ant, "you can eat all you want, no problem. It's just that the lion is about to arrive, and all these crops are his. I planted them for him because he ordered me to."

The elephant went away. A few days later the lion came by and he too asked the ant for a bite to eat.

The ant addressed the king of the jungle, "Eat all you want, Mr. Lion, but the elephant is about to arrive to harvest his crops. He paid me to plant all of them." So the lion trudged off. And that is how the ant was able to enjoy his crops for himself.

"That's called give-and-take, negotiating," concluded Bambara Keita's grandfather.

The African returned to the present. He had to concentrate, and to do so he needed to take these brief mental trips back to his village. That's it. He had to return to his childhood to remember his elder's advice. At that moment he needed his guidance more than ever.

"I thought I could write a contract for a household assistant, and you could use that contract to legalize your status," Montse offered.

For a moment Bambara Keita had forgotten about the pain he was feeling over his friend's death, the one who had accompanied him on his journey to Spain. He needed to focus on the present because he was now in the process of negotiating.

"So what do you think of that idea?"

Montse sensed that the African was a little uneasy as he considered it. Was it that the term "household assistant" offended him? Bambara Keita did not answer for awhile. He was designing a verbal contract, but the women didn't know it.

"Aren't you going to answer, Bambara Keita?"

This time it was Roser who impatiently asked the question. She feared that he was quiet because he had possibly gotten a better offer. She didn't know why, but for the first time it occurred to her that the African might abandon them. But why was that? It's remarkable how we only appreciate the value of people or things when we think we're going to lose them. Her head was spinning. If they had come up with this idea, who could be sure that other women in the same city and in the same situation were not thinking the same thing? People walk carefree through the streets, thinking proudly that they don't have any problems or needs. But just like Roser and Montse, people had problems. She was sure that there were others living double lives, their neighbors oblivious. What's more, Bambara Keita was now well dressed and his tall figure made him stand out. More than a few women would surely take note of him.

"Household assistant," murmured Bambara Keita, wondering if he should be offended by the title.

He considered his long, painful quest to reach the promised land of the whites, as well as the months of intense work for his patrons. His experience had taught him a great deal.

"It's just a name. Not important," Roser added. "It's just so you can get your documents. All three of us know that's not your real work."

Montse looked intently at her friend. For the first time Roser displayed a cooperative attitude.

Meanwhile the African continued his attempt to cut a deal. After a moment he asked them exactly what a household assistant was. He pretended not to know the meaning of the term. But perhaps he wanted to explain it to himself. So he continued negotiating the contract.

"Well, it's like what we explained to you before. It's like being a butler—you're the one in charge of the house's upkeep."

Roser, once again, had her own idea. Montse was surprised by the sudden change in her friend's disposition.

Bambara Keita was now fully engaged and murmured, "Well, if you want, I say yes."

Roser took a deep breath before Montse responded, "Fine, I'll find out what documents we need."

But Bambara Keita knew what they needed, and he told them, adding that he would like to go to Madrid to file for a passport. His precision made the two friends nervous.

"But your passport is already being processed," said Montse.

Bambara Keita recognized that the most difficult part of the negotiations had arrived. He knew it would come. He truly wished he could postpone this moment as long as possible. He had spent sleepless nights thinking about it. After making love with his lover-bosses, his eyes would stay open as they slept. At the beginning of their relationship, it did not bother him. But as their relationship grew, his anguish did too. He tried to remember all of his grandfather's stories, but none of them seemed applicable to his present situation. They didn't seem to contain the wisdom he needed to confront this situation. However, his grandfather's words were still deeply embedded in him. "Life is about getting what you need by giving a little and taking a little," he heard his elder's encouragement. And now that the moment of agreement had arrived, he had to continue to negotiate. He had no choice.

"I must tell truth." He lowered his head like a child who had just done something wrong. He asked them to forgive him. He said he did it because he was helpless, desperate. And now there was no other way out.

The women listened to him with both curiosity and concern. Roser seemed more worried than Montse.

"What happened, Bambara Keita?" asked Roser, trying to appear calm.

The African continued staring at the ground, avoiding their gaze. This time it had nothing to do with his loyalty to tradition. He was bargaining his way out.

"Why aren't you answering, Bambara Keita? What happened," asked Montse.

"I lie. I no tell truth."

None of the explanations the African had conjured up in preparation for this moment were adequate. Before he had been holding out for something better, making it seem as though he had an ace in the hole when he really had nothing. That was why he wanted them to think he was self-confident. But now it was different. Now he was no longer at an advantage. So he opted for pity. Yes, he had to make his bosses feel sorry for him.

He told them that while he was crossing into Europe a few bad men had attacked him and his travel companions. They had robbed him of everything, including his passport. He explained sorrowfully that when he got to Melilla, he managed to earn a little money and buy a passport.

But he had made the story up at that very moment. He had never though about it before. He didn't know if it would be convincing. Finally understanding that the problem was just with his passport, Roser sighed with relief. But Montse was still worried and asked, "So the passport you have is not yours?"

The African shook his head, still facing the floor. When he was a boy, he told them, whenever he had a problem, his father, grandfather, or even his female family members, would always say, "Men don't cry." Crying showed weakness, it was what women did. But at the same time, wasn't weakness precisely what made people feel sorry for others?

He was always considering his elders' advice, because at times they were warnings. A male son can always aspire to become the head of the clan. But he knew at that moment he was far from his clan, and far from his people. They wouldn't see him cry. And he figured that if his grandfather had seen him cry, he'd know he was following his advice. So he didn't hold back the tears. In fact, he wanted to let the women see them. But for some reason those tears refused to come out, probably because his elders' advice was ingrained in him. He tried to recall the harshness of his life through all those years, the treacherous trip to Spain. He thought of the day Montse found him in the Plaza de Cataluña. After living in those conditions, under such dire circumstances, shedding tears should not have been so difficult. He squeezed his eyes, coaxing out the tears.

"Not my passport, someone else passport. I not from Mali but Cameroon."

The two women looked at each other. Nothing they'd heard made any difference as far as their plan was concerned, even though Bambara Keita's revelation had surprised them. They hadn't expected it. Actually, they didn't know exactly what to expect. Montse observed that the man's eyes were red. They knew he was feeling bad about it, that he was about to shed tears, or was actually crying. But they couldn't see his face clearly. The person they had known until then was a man who lifted his head just enough to let them see the sad expression in his eyes. But then he looked down again.

"Well, that's not so bad," Montse tried to encourage him.

The African continued where he had left off. He told himself it was time to seal the transaction..

"I sorry," he said. He told them dejectedly that he didn't want to lie, that he only did it because he was not legal. He continued playing the victim as they came to an agreement.

"So your name is not Bambara Keita, right?" Roser said this more as a statement than a question. The Black man did not reply immediately.

"I Gerard Essomba from Ebolowa, Cameroon," he let it out in one breath, almost without thinking. His tone was weak, repentant, because he was still negotiating. He knew that he had not completely convinced them. He had no idea what these two women's reaction would be when they discovered the farce. So he decided to continue without hesitation. Deep down he was relieved, most of all because he had just shed a heavy burden. He thought he heard the voice of his grandfather telling him, "Very good, Gerard Essomba, you have done very well!" For once, after such a long time, he heard his real name slip through his lips.

If it had been difficult to assume the identity of another man, it was even more difficult to usurp that man's nationality. He had to make lots of things up. He had never been to Mali. On his journey he had passed through Senegal, but he had never entered the country of that legendary wise man, Amadou Hampaté Bâ, or of the soccer star, Salif Keïta

In his negotiations, the newly revealed Gerard Essomba realized that the truth that had just come out of his mouth had given him utmost peace. Now the lies he had conjured up for all that time were not important to him, like he and his friends being robbed in the Sahara Desert. None of that had happened.

At one point on his long journey to Europe, someone in the know had informed him and his companions that it was essential to hide your real identity in the land of the whites. Especially in Spain, which would be the first stop. He got rid of every document that would connect him with his real country, so that if the police ever arrested him, they could not deport him to his nation of origin.

This advice turned out to be useful to him. His attempt to reach Spain had been successful largely due to the fact that no one was able to prove his country of origin. Because he lacked a home country, the authorities had nowhere to deport him to, and they simply set him free in the streets of Barcelona. The ones who didn't hide their national identity were deported. It was true that he had acquired his passport when he was in Melilla, but he always kept it hidden. Even in Barcelona, he never had it with him. He had wrapped his false passport in a plastic bag and hidden it in a hole in the pavement on the Plaza de Cataluña.

"Gerard Essomba!" exclaimed Montse.

The African came out of the stupor of his thoughts. He jolted when he heard his real name from the woman's lips. She had pronounced it correctly. My God, that name belonged to him! He felt something he had never felt before. He still had no idea how his boss-lovers would react, but no matter their reaction, it could not erase the feelings of relief he felt at that moment. It was as if he had been born again, as if suddenly he had regained his sense of self, his hometown and his clan. He began to live again. How many know the anguish of having to respond to another's name and identity? He, Gerard Essomba, the ex-Bambara Keita—yes, he had felt it.

He didn't know why, but when he heard Montse use his real name, he recalled an episode from his boyhood. It involved his mother. He remembered that once, when he had been playing soccer with his friends in the big town, his mother had called to him from their dwelling and told him to fetch water from the brook. He had pretended not to hear her, but suddenly, without any warning, he felt someone pinch his ear. His mother came over to him without him noticing and grabbed his ear from behind. She dragged him into the kitchen without a thought to how much his ear hurt.

"Gerard Essomba, if you don't go and fetch me water right this instant, you'll see what happens to you!" she declared as she shoved a bucket into his hand.

Later, his grandfather, who had watched the entire scene, said, "You have to obey when you're asked to do something." That's all he said.

Montse's voice made him think of his mother, even though she didn't sound like the woman who had given birth to him. She had pronounced his name perfectly, just like his mom.

"So what should we do?" Roser asked hesitantly.

"Nothing has changed," Montse assured. "Well not exactly nothing. His home country has changed. And his name. So the man we thought was named Bambara Keita is actually Gerard Essomba. Well... But he's the same guy. So death to Bambara Keita, and long live Gerard Essomba!" she asserted sarcastically.

Roser was unsure about the whole thing. She looked at the African. He was still reluctant to show them his full face. He felt inner peace, but he also realized that he had to keep negotiating. His role as the victim still had to remain a priority.

"How do we know that you're telling the truth now?" Roser was still skeptical.

The African knew what to do to convince them. He got up and showed them an ID card. He told them that this was the identification he used to send his family money when they paid him. The ID was from Cameroon. He made sure to stress that *they* were the ones who made it possible for him to send money home. He was making a deal. He knew that demonstrating their benevolence would touch their hearts.

In fact, he was now negotiating from a disadvantage. They had to know that if it weren't for them he would never have been able to regain his real identity. It was their doing, and that was important. White people like to know that the progress of Black people and other "inferiors" is due to their generous efforts. Gerard Essombo was poor but he was not stupid. He knew a lot, maybe too much, about what white people wanted, and most of all about what they expected from Blacks. But more than anything, he knew the skill of entering into a contract.

Montse was the first to examine the card he was handing them. She read it to herself. There was a color photo that had been taken in Spain. The African had not been wrong. She knew she had helped him send money to his family. She felt proud. It had been a great act of charity. Or, perhaps it had been what people in Catalonia preferred to call it—solidarity.

After studying the document she handed it to Roser. Roser gave it a brief glance and handed it back to its owner. Something had caught her attention.

"Let me see it again."

He gave it back to her, and Roser looked at it again.

"So you say your relatives had this done for you after you arrived in Spain?"

"Yes," he assured, and added again that he sent them money when they paid him. The man who was once Bambara Keita knew that the negotiations were still going on, despite their preliminary agreement. He couldn't let go. He couldn't proclaim victory yet.

"So if you were here, how did they get your fingerprints?"

The man didn't understand what she was asking.

"Fingerprints?" he asked, not knowing how to pronounce Roser's word.

"This—" Roser showed him the part of the card with the finger-prints. Montse also noticed it.

"I didn't see that," she said. "How did they do it?"

The African said sincerely that he had not noticed either.

"What? You mean those prints aren't yours?"

The African replied that they must be some other person's prints.

"How can they be some other person's?" asked Roser. "You mean that in your country just anyone can have their fingerprints stamped on any document?"

"In Cameroon that possible." The African explained the practices of his country. He told them that over there, you could easily bribe someone in public office. "Corruption," he said. "Africa much corruption," pronouncing the word both with difficulty and certainty.

But the man had lost the small bit of hope he had just acquired. He was fearful once again. That little detail might cost him his place in paradise. There was nothing to do but go back to the negotiating table, and from a disadvantage, as usual. He looked at his questioners, knowing they were doubting him. So he elaborated on his previous explanation. With all the clarity and eloquence he could muster in his African Spanish, he told them that in his country stealing was common across society: the police, the military, the government. And since people in Cameroon did not enjoy the fruits of a democracy like the one in which they were living, no one could say anything to question it. Nothing, he reiterated. "Cameroon, very bad," he insisted. "We come to Spain for law, justice, good society."

His voice had again adopted the tone of humility and sadness that he had begun with. He looked down, but not without noticing how his bosses were responding to his words. His grandfather's voice was still in his head, and God's was there too. He thought that at this moment he needed God more than his grandfather. Or did he need them both?

"But really, tell the truth: are you from Cameroon? Because with all that corruption you're talking about, how do we know you aren't part of it? You could have bought that ID and nationality," Montse said sarcastically. As usual, she was the first to respond.

The immigrant also reacted quickly. He saw they were still skeptical, so did what he could to allay their doubts. "I from Cameroon, by God. No lie." He had not told the truth before, he said, because he did not have documentation. "I go Madrid, get passport now, no problem."

In spite of being from the Catalan upper class and having relatives who were firmly Catholic, Montse was not religious. So when someone told her they were swearing in the name of God, it didn't mean much to her. She had her own way of understanding life and people. Still, what the African was saying touched her. It seemed unnecessary to humiliate the poor guy.

"Alright, we believe you," she said. "So go to Madrid to get your passport."

Roser said nothing.

"But don't lie to us again," she advised.

"I no lie now. You know truth."

Those last words sounded to Montse like a plea. He had just told them one of his life's secrets. At that moment they held his life in their hands. Montse sympathized with his anguish.

"Fine, but now I don't know what to call you," she said, in order to change the subject and inject a little humor. "I was used to Bambara Keita. I liked it." She saw shame on his face, so was quick to add, "But Gerard Essomba is a nice name too. I like it just as much. And since it's your real name, I'll start to use it. What should I say? Gerard, Essomba, or both together?"

With a little bit of shame still showing on his face, he shrugged his shoulders.

"I'll use both."

"I like your other name, so I'll keep on calling you Bambara Keita. We'll see," said Roser.

"Roser, haven't we already declared death to Bambara Keita, and long life to Gerard Essomba?" asked Montse.

"Yes, but it's hard to get used to."

"Just try to use it. You'll grow accustomed."

Roser had dinner with them, and then she went home. Gerard Essomba, after brushing his teeth, went to his room. He was relaxed, and Montse was still puttering around in the kitchen. Standing in his room, he began to pray to God. He thanked Him for the path that had opened for him. He prayed for a long and blessed life for the two women, because they were good. Yes, he thought, there are good people in this world. Really good people. Those two women understood his problems, his pain, his misfortune. In spite of all the lies he had told them, they forgave him for his crude falsehoods.

"Lord, who but You could fix things for a servant of yours like me? To open up a path for me like this one?" he prayed. He also asked Him to have mercy on his fallen friend's soul. "You must know, my God, why you called him so soon," he murmured in his prayer. He called himself a sinner, along with all the people in the world. Gerard Essomba believed that the misfortunes people suffered were their own doing. They deserved it for having offended God. Although he could never quite explain how or why humans were able to offend God. When he opened his eyes he saw Montse sitting next to him on the bed. He was concentrating so intently on his prayer that he hadn't heard her come in.

"I no hear you." He tried to smile.

"I tried to make a little noise. I guess you were far away from this world. I thought maybe you were in heaven," she laughed.

"No laugh, I say thanks God. I no tell truth before, but now I say who I am."

Montse recognized his pain, the hurt of a man obligated to assume another man's name and identity. A tenderness had entered her heart.

"Come here."

He moved close to her and kissed her passionately. Gerard Essomba lowered his head toward her breasts and buried it between them. Montse caressed the part of his head left uncovered by her breasts. That maternal affection pleased him. He began to kiss her nipples. At that moment he had an irresistible urge to possess her. He slipped off the bed and knelt in front of her, and from that position he moved his face between her legs. From that position it was not easy to reach Montse's vagina. He grabbed her legs and lifted them, coaxing her to lie face up on the bed. He did this with all his might. He was crazed with desire. He didn't think he could possibly lift all her weight. But he was not in the mood for uncertainties. He moved toward the foot of the bed and opened her legs. Even in this position it was not easy to expose her entire vulva. But he didn't care. He immersed his head between her legs and let his tongue go searching for her fleshy vagina. The scent of it invaded his lungs while he sucked vigorously, searching for the way so that he could go deeper and deeper with his tongue.

"Déu meu!" she cried, vibrating with pleasure. "I can't live without you, my love. Oh God, what delight!" she screamed.

Her entire body was trembling, leading up to one shocking jolt. She closed her legs, and without meaning to, she almost choked her lover. Gerard Essomba finally managed, not without difficulty, to free his head from between her legs and breathe deeply. But that little obstacle had not lessened his desire. He had never before desired a woman as he did that day. He took off his pajamas and signaled for Montse to turn around so that he could enter her from behind. Montse got on her knees and offered him her entire ass. The sight of it made the man from Cameroon crazy. He hesitated for a moment. He placed his head between his lover's haunches and vagina. With nearly his entire head and half his neck hidden between Montse's thighs, vagina, and hips, Gerard Essomba sucked up all the juices he found down there. Montse could not take it any longer—another orgasm made her lose control of her legs and the rest of her body. She tumbled onto the man's head as she screamed out for the God she did not believe in, as if she wanted him to bear witness to her unique pleasure. Gasping for breath, Gerard Essomba once again managed to free his head and help Montse get back into her previous position. Now she let him have his way. The African plowed into her with all of his force, just the way she liked it. The woman let out a last shriek as her torso landed again on the bed. Just like the first time they had been together, they lay there without moving. She was breathing rapidly, and he did what he could to keep his balance with his penis still inside her.

After awhile, Montse showed signs of life, as she began to move around the bed as usual. It was a sign that her young lover knew well. Little by little he lifted his body to get back into position. Between her pleasure and pain, it seemed to her that the man's prick had gotten bigger than ever that night. She was sure she had never felt such strength, even though he had done what he always did. Later on, as he slept, she slid her hands between his legs to find his shaft. Indeed, it was him. She turned on the lamp and contemplated his face. He looked as he always did—it was him. She couldn't keep herself from giving him a kiss on the face. She turned out the light and slept.

CHAPTER 11

ERARD ESSOMBA, THE EX-BAMBARA KEITA, traveled to Madrid and returned a few days later with his passport in order, along with the rest of the documentation he needed. Processing his residency application and his work permit was not difficult. Montse had referred him to a lawyer who worked for her company. A month and a half after he presented the pertinent documents and applications, the African received his papers. He couldn't suppress his happiness since the day he obtained the receipt proving he had submitted the application. He finally felt like an authentic human being. He could walk freely down the city's streets without having to hide from the police. When he came across a person in authority—a policeman or a government official—he no longer felt the anguish that had come over him before. The day he received his documentation he invited his friends out. He was elated.

When the two women learned of their African's legalization, they were relieved. This also allowed him to come and go from their apartments without fear of the immigration authorities. The doorman at Montse's, building knew him, although he only worked during the daytime. At night Montse brought him in secretly, and when he left he had to do so early in the morning, before anyone was up. On weekends and holidays, when it was her turn to have him, they never left the apartment. But with Roser, things were different. He entered her place very cautiously, and on the following day he left in the early hours, like anyone who had to get to work.

Everything went well until the day the head of Roser's company called her into his office.

"Ms. Calatabuig," said Mr. Koffman, the CEO, after Roser sat down. "As you know, the company is extremely pleased with you. Your work is marvelous. I'll get to the point. The directors have decided to send you to Berlin for two years."

"To Berlin?" She was not expecting this.

"Yes, Ms. Calatabuig, we've opened a new office there, and we think with your experience you are the ideal person for the job."

Mr. Koffman was a big man. He had an enormous round face and wore partially tinted glasses that hid his eyes. Roser stared at him, trying to discern his expression. She thought he was joking.

"Mr. Koffman, that would mean I'd have to leave my life here." She couldn't think of anything else to say.

"That's no longer an issue these days. That's the way things are. I too left my home in Germany."

"It's not the same."

"Why don't you think it's the same?" He asked in a pleasant voice, a smile on his face.

Roser wanted to tell him that Barcelona was not at all like Berlin, but she thought that might be undiplomatic, so she spoke instead about the climate, people, and customs.

"You have it better than I did," added the German executive. "You speak German very well, you travel there regularly on business, and you even lived there for awhile. When I arrived here three years ago, on the other hand, I did not speak Spanish, and even less Catalan."

"But really, it's still not the same. I lived there a few years when I was younger. But now—"

The German didn't let her finish. "But Señora Calatabuig, you are still young, and Germany is much nicer now than when you lived there. I think you'll agree."

Roser remained silent for a moment. Of course she knew there was going to be a new office in Berlin, but she hadn't imagined that she would be the unfortunate one to have to go there.

"And when do you want me to be there?" She'd given up arguing with him.

"Today is Monday, and you need to be in your new office by no later than Wednesday of next week."

"So soon? I won't have time to get everything ready!"

"You may have the rest of this week off."

End of conversation.

Roser left the executive's office. When she was back in her own office, she thought about her situation. She didn't know how she was going to deal with this turn of events. She kept thinking about it on the way home. Leaving for Germany would mean she would have to abandon everything that she had in Barcelona—her family, friends, and of course her employee-lover, Gerard Essomba, a.k.a. Bambara Keita. Thinking about the African, her heart began to beat rapidly. She realized she had a problem. How would she tell Montse? What was she going to do?

Montse had told her one day that all her ills came from lack of sex.

"The truth is that I've been feeling much better lately too, less irritable—almost not at all—and no more anxiety," Roser had replied.

A week after that conversation, they got rid of all the mood stabilizers in their houses. They both swore they would never get themselves into that situation again, that they would never suffer from sex starvation. Even if the one they knew then as Bambara Keita left, they would find someone else. They had the means, and money can solve all problems.

Roser was perplexed about the future. She was not as bold as her friend. She wasn't as sure of herself. She was simply not as capable of executing a plan like the one Montse had conjured up—successfully! No one in the city had any idea about their double lives. At least no one they were aware of.

Roser tried to conceive of her new life in Germany. Berlin was beautiful, but dull. She went through all the German cities she knew: Frankfurt, Hamburg, Freiburg, Heidelberg, Offenburg, others. She thought about the one she liked the most. They were all pretty, but to her, they were boring. The cities were as cold as the people who inhabited them. If she had been that bored there when she was young, what would they be like now? As much as Koffman had tried to convince her that Germany had changed, she did not believe it. Maybe the cities were different now, but surely not the people. They were still robot-like. She knew it, she worked with them.

She imagined herself in Berlin with Gerard Essomba. She smiled slyly to herself. "Well, maybe," she murmured. She also tried to imagine her life without the African. A deep sadness overcame her. *God, I love him*, she heard a voice cry out from inside her. Damn, she had to arrive at the possibility of leaving him to realize she was in love. It was no longer just sex, she had fallen for that Black man. She suddenly understood why she was in a bad mood when he was not in her house: because it was Montse's turn to have him. It was jealousy. "Oh, how horrible!" She was horrified by her discovery. But it was true. She was ashamed of herself. *Look at me*, she thought, *I'm jealous of my best friend because of a Black man!* She tried to get that absurd thought out of her head and concentrate on her new situation. But as she thought about it, she realized the image of the African immigrant kept making its way into her mind. When she included the African in her future, her attitude toward her new destination changed. She no longer had any doubts. But how could she convince him to come with her to Germany? And if she convinced him, what would he do there? Montse needed him as much as she did. Maybe she was in love with him too. An intense melancholy invaded her. If she asked Montse to let her go to Germany with the African, she was sure she would not like it. And persuading the African to go off with her to Berlin without telling her friend would be a betrayal. *What do I do?*

That night she went to bed without eating dinner. She couldn't manage to sleep. Luckily Gerard Essomba wouldn't be with her for the next few days. For the first time ever, she actually preferred his absence. She needed to think things through and put things in order.

The next day she still wasn't able wrap her mind around the situation, no matter how much she tried. Every now and then she thought she had resolved it, but moments later she would throw herself on the couch, utterly perplexed, deep in doubt. As morning broke the following day, after having tossed and turned all night, she came to a decision. It was the one she least wanted, but there was no other choice. She concluded she simply couldn't leave without her man. She would try to convince him to come with her, risking the loss of her friendship with Montse. But she couldn't do anything else. No, nothing else was possible.

Tuesday evening Montse called to ask what was going on with her. Roser answered as if nothing was happening. She decided that her first priority was that no one should find out. She would tell her mother and father when she got to Germany. It was not a good solution, but her mother might be indiscreet. No, no one was going to know. She was going to wait for the African to arrive the following day to explain the whole thing to him. She had already prepared what she was going to say. Although she was still uneasy, slowly she tried to order her future life. She thought about the clothes she would bring, the music.

On Wednesday afternoon, Montse called to invite her to dinner.

"I'll buy one of those roast chickens you like so much, and the Penedés wine I know you like."

Roser tried to get out of it. She needed to avoid coming face to face with Montse.

"I'm tired. I'm not sure if I can make it, Montse."

"Bah! What's a little weariness with a chicken on your plate and a glass of local red wine? Come on, girl, I'll see you at nine!" She did not wait for a response.

Roser closed her eyes. If she didn't go, Montse would probably come over to her place with the meal. That's the way she was! Montse was such a good friend and good person. Roser shook her head , and then brought her hand to her face. Montse's generous invitation brought back her sadness. Why did it have to be that way? Why was life so complicated? When you think you've got everything figured out, something happens and ruins it all. And suddenly a lasting sisterly friendship breaks.

"My God, what can I do?" she sighed. Although she was a believer, she knew at times heaven gives you no indication, and when you asked sometimes you got nothing in reply.

The possibility of finding herself in front of Montse sunk her even more. She stopped everything she was doing and fell into bed. She closed her eyes, hoping to find an answer. A minute later she opened her eyes, and all she saw was the ceiling of her bedroom. She knew the true solution had to come from her. It all depended on her actions. She finally decided she would go to Montse's for dinner, there was no other way. She would try to be true to herself.

A little after nine thirty, Roser was ringing Montse's doorbell. As she waited, she shut her eyes. Time stopped. She thought she was ready for it, but she suddenly realized she wasn't. She was about to turn around and leave, but just as that absurd idea crossed her mind, the door opened.

"Roser, bravo!" Montse enthusiastically embraced her. Roser forced a smile and accepted Montse's kisses.

"Come right in, we've been waiting! I thought you wouldn't come. I was about to call, and I had already told Gerard Essomba that if you didn't show up, we'd take the chicken over to your place." Just as Roser had imagined.

"I was pretty tired, I've been working very hard," she said, trying to initiate a conversation.

"Overworking. It's what our society demands, but you can easily counter it with good food and friends," Montse announced as she pulled her friend into the dining room. The African had taken a seat on the sofa. He stood up to greet the new arrival. Roser couldn't look him in the eye.

"Hola Roser," he said.

"Hola," she answered dryly.

"Let's eat before the chicken gets cold," said the host.

After they sat down, Montse announced, "You do look tired."

"I told you I've had a crazy day, but I'm feeling a little better now. I'm getting over it," she lied.

"Don't let those Germans squeeze the life out of you, girl. They say that they work like robots over there."

"Well, yes, some of them."

It was difficult for Roser to eat. For two days she had only been drinking liquids.

"Listen, Roser, I had you over here for a reason," Montse started. Roser felt like something long and sharp was striking at her heart. Trying to alleviate the feeling, she gulped down her wine.

"You know how happy I get when spring arrives. It's the time of year that lifts me from my rut and gives me energy. I can't help it.

That's why I thought we need to get started planning our summer together; it's just around the corner, as they say." She stopped talking because Roser was coughing. Roser got up immediately and went to the bathroom. Montse followed her.

"What's the matter with you?" Roser couldn't answer right away. She continued coughing.

"It's nothing," she tried to say, gasping for breath. "I've just choked on something."

Roser saw Montse in the mirror. She looked at her and at herself. Montse put her hand on her shoulder.

"Well don't choke now. Wait until you hear my proposal."

Roser's eyes were red. There were a few tears running down her cheeks. She was crying. If only she could be alone now! She turned on the faucet and washed her face so that they wouldn't notice. Finally, she was able to compose herself.

"Let's go back to the dining room. I'm okay," she told Montse.

The African, not knowing what was going on, continued eating.

"Well, as I was saying, I thought this summer we could go to Greece."

"Greece?" asked Roser.

"Well, I don't know where exactly, but like I said, spring brings me hope and happiness. Why? Well, I guess I thought it might interest both of you. I also thought about Portugal. I love Lisbon, but I'm afraid we might just run into someone we know there. But if you've got other ideas..."

"No, it's okay. I was just asking because you took me by surprise."

"Gerard Essomba, what do you think of the idea? Would you like to see an ancient country like Greece?" asked Montse.

"Oh yes," he said, and as usual he tried to entertain his women by including a story with his answer. He told them about a teacher he had in Cameroon who said that the Greeks had traveled to Egypt in search of the wisdom of the ruling pharaohs, who were Black. These were his ancestors, he explained. Then the Greeks brought that wisdom back to Europe. Many Africans believe that ancient culture from Greece comes from Africa. Egypt, he said, is where the Greeks got their philosophy, but that fact had been erased by history. The African spoke with a tone of pride that didn't go unnoticed by the two women, who stared at each other, wondering what he was talking about.

"Is that right?" Roser asked, now forgetting about her own dilemma.

"Yes," announced Gerard Essomba, "in Egypt all Black people."

"I'd never heard that, at least not the way you tell it," said Montse.

"That's right," he said, believing he was teaching his listeners something new.

"Well then, we'll go to Greece and you'll discover the country whose people went to rob knowledge from your ancestors, as you say," she joked.

"But Greeks no go to steal, they go to learn."

All the talk about Greece and Egypt relieved Roser's nervousness.

"Whatever you say, but what we can count on is that you'll see it," said Roser, pleased that she wasn't arousing any suspicion.

"So tomorrow I'll go to a travel agency. I hope it's not too late. We'll need two rooms, a double for us and a single for our man. What do you think?" Montse asked Roser.

"Fine."

"You don't look very convinced. If you'd rather go some place else..."

"No, not at all," Roser insisted. "It's just that I'm very tired. I think I'll go to bed early. Go ahead and get the information. I'll ask around too."

"Alright, no more talk! In August we'll visit the Greeks, the first Europeans to discover there was something to learn on the other side of the Mediterranean," Montse said, looking mischievously at the African. "You've barely touched your dinner! You must have had a truly horrid day. You usually love roasted chicken." Montse accompanied her friend to the door.

"It was very good. It's just that I'm tired."

Montse bid her farewell and went back into her apartment.,As Roser approached the elevator, no longer in Montse's sight, she couldn't hold it in any longer. Tears streamed down her face. She rushed out the elevator and ran to her car. When she was inside she began to sob desperately and loudly. Her entire body convulsed. She barely had the strength to start the car. She sat in the seat, unable to calm herself. An hour later she drove home.

CHAPTER 12

ROSER GREW NERVOUS WAITING FOR Gerard Essomba in her apartment. It was Thursday, and the African had called to ask what time she expected him. She said to come at the same time as usual, about eleven in the evening. Roser looked at her clock. It was ten thirty. She had rehearsed what she was going say, but—like a schoolgirl studying for an exam—she had forgotten the words she'd memorized.

Who would have known that she, Roser Calatabuig Pons, was going to find herself all tangled up with a Black man? She discarded that last thought quickly, but she acknowledged she had never lived through anything like what she was going through now.

She had married when she was young. The marriage didn't even last three years. Her ex-husband was old-fashioned: he remained anchored to a past in which a good woman obeyed and didn't do much else. She was no longer part of that generation. When Franco died, she was still young. She had just gone through adolescence, and she yearned for the liberty that Spanish women were looking for.

She separated from her husband despite the objections of her parents. They were conservatives who didn't even want to hear the word divorce. From then on, she swore that no man would ever tell her what to do or use her to his advantage. And since that time, that was how she lived. Every now and then she'd have a random affair, but if a man wanted a stable, long-term relationship, Roser immediately showed him the door.

With the years, her affairs became more infrequent and more difficult. She didn't have as many options as before. And in the middle of all this emotional chaos, Montse came along and cooked up her phantasmagorical plan of bringing a Black man into her home and bed. What she considered a simple diversion had turned into a weighty burden. Without wanting or expecting it, she found herself trapped in an absurd situation. Despite her awareness of her dilemma, she had no way to solve it outside of betraying her best friend and humiliating herself. Roser knew what she was doing. She knew she was not behaving well: she should not deal her friend such a bad hand, but she saw no other way out.

At a quarter past eleven, the building intercom rang. She knew it was him, he didn't have to announce himself. But she did what she usually did when he rang from the front door. She asked him what he wanted, in case a neighbor was listening. When the African uttered the password indicating he was alone, she pressed the button to let him in the building.

Roser met Gerard Essomba at the door to her apartment. In spite of his youth and inexperience with whites, he knew something wasn't right. She was sucking on her cigarette with greater intensity than usual, with shorter, more frequent puffs. Roser was nervous.

"Have you had dinner?"

"Yes, I eat at home."

The African had already sat down on the sofa. She sat in a chair across from him.

"I've got something important to tell you Bambara—I mean Gerard Essomba," she corrected herself and feigned a smile. "Sorry, I just can't get used to it."

"No worry." He knew there was something wrong with this woman. He smiled back to try to calm her down.

"I have a problem and I'd like to tell you about it. But before I tell you, I want you to swear that you won't tell anyone."

The African nodded.

"No, Gerard Essomba, that's not enough! I want you to swear in God's name that you won't tell absolutely anyone what I'm going to say, not even Montse!" she tried to be as clear as possible.

The African was perplexed, but he did what he was told. He swore by God that not even Montse would know. But Roser was not convinced.

"Remember, you've already given me your word you won't tell anyone."

"I swear, I tell truth," the African repeated.

"Look," she began, "my company, I mean my work, is sending me to Germany."

"Oh, Germany!" The African's expression was filled with admiration, as well as uneasiness about the possibility that his good fortune might be coming to an end.

"Yes, I'm going to Germany, and that's just what I want to talk to you about. I want you to come and live with me there." Roser uttered that last sentence as if her desire had been a great burden, and now that she expressed it, she was relieved. The African was silent.

"Do you hear what I'm saying, Gerard Essomba?" she asked, impatient with his apparent passivity.

"Yes, I hear." Gerard knew that it was time to negotiate again, but he wasn't sure exactly what. All he was certain of was the fact that his interlocutor wanted to include him in her trip, and that meant another deal. Again he recalled his grandfather's wisdom, and he was quick to tell Roser about it. When the hen sees many corn kernels on the ground, he related, she would peck hard and fast, and when she picked them all up, she would pause to enjoy it. And that was just what he was doing. He was listening intently to what she was saying, but now it was time to consider it carefully. Roser was fed up with his grandfather

and the rest of them, she would have sent them all to hell. *Lord,
this is too much!* she said to herself. But she didn't express this.

"So look, Montse was the one who found you, and I was against
it. But as this has gone on, I've become accustomed to it. I'm liking
it more and more. And right now, I love you very much. But there
is a problem, and not just because they're sending me to Germany.
I don't think our situation here can last much longer. It's a matter
of time before people will begin to notice. Montse is part of a
prominent family, not just here in Barcelona but in all of Spain.
My family is known, but not like Montse's. Mine is more modest.
If Montse's family ever found out that she was going out with a
Black man, they'd either make her cut the relationship off or try
to eliminate you."

The African heard the word eliminate, but he was not quite sure
what she meant. "Kill me you mean?"

"Don't worry, that's just a manner of speaking." she said, and
with that she saw that the African was relieved. "What I mean is
that an amorous relationship between a woman of Montse's class
with a man like you just won't be accepted."

"So what now?" he asked, still uneasy.

Roser again saw fear in his eyes. That fear gave her the confidence to continue. She knew she was on the right path. She was not
lying. Despite her betrayal, she wanted to be honest with him. She
felt she needed to use the right words to make him less anxious.

"So now you are not like the hen, you're more like the duck.
You're not pecking to enjoy it later."

The African realized that he had fallen into a contradiction.
"You right, I listen."

Roser didn't speak right away. She was convinced she wasn't
on the wrong path. Little by little, she was releasing her burden.
She knew what she told him was true, that if people found out

there would be consequences. They were living a double life with him, but that could all come to halt, which would be a disaster.

"So I'm proposing that you come with me to Germany. We can get married, if you want. In a couple of years you could request Spanish citizenship and get a passport from the European Union. With that you could go anywhere. And if one day you no longer want to be married to me, you can divorce me, but you'll still have all your documents from the European Union." The African was about to say something. "Wait, I haven't finished! I'm going to make you another proposition. You told me you'd love to build a pretty house in your town. Okay. So in a few years I'll go with you to Cameroon, and we'll build that house together. I'll contribute, so that when it's done it'll belong to both of us." She smiled. "That's what I wanted to propose to you. I don't want to obligate you to do anything. Today is Thursday, so I'll let you think about it until Saturday, because if you accept we'll have to leave here on Monday. If you say no, it'll be all right. The only thing I ask is that you don't breathe a word of this to Montse."

Roser was greatly relieved. She looked at her African. He tried to say something, but she cut him off. "Please, don't say anything now. Think it over before you give me an answer. You know you have until Saturday to decide." He was silent. "Would you like anything to eat or drink?"

She offered this mostly as a way to relieve the tension. Gerard Essomba accepted her offer. "Anything," he said.

"How about a glass of wine?" she suggested as she brought out a bottle. He accepted indifferently. She poured and they drank in silence. For as hard as they tried to feign that everything was normal, something strange had come between them. Suddenly they seemed afraid of each another.

"Shall we go to bed?"

"Yes."

They got into bed, but it was the same there. The man made no move toward her, and neither did she toward him. Gerard Essomba tried to think, but he couldn't. He couldn't sleep either. He knew the same thing was happening to his companion.

The next day he left Roser's apartment as usual at the hour that any house servant leaves their employer's house after work. He went to his own place and threw himself into bed. In his own dwelling it was easier for him to think. He pondered Roser's offer. It was not the first time a woman had proposed to him. His lover from Cameroon had asked several times, but he declined. He didn't want to do anything like that before realizing his great dream, the dream he shared with so many of his generation, as well as the ones before him and even the generations to come: to arrive at the destination, the land of the whites. To reach Paradise. When he embarked on his journey he hadn't even told her, or his mother and father. They didn't know where he had gone until four years later, after his arrival to Barcelona.

In any case, this was not the same. He couldn't compare his ex-girlfriend to Roser. Roser was an elegant lady—classy, high society, white, and rich. He tried to weigh the pros and cons. Roser wasn't like Montse. It's true that Montse didn't have the most attractive body. It was too big, too much flesh. But she was affectionate, sensitive, and generous. Not a week went by when she did not surprise him with a gift. All the expensive clothes he owned were presents from her. She had given him a brand-name wristwatch, as well as the gold chain around his neck.

And besides all that, she was extraordinarily clean. She always smelled beautifully. True, she was fat, but she had a pretty face. Her skin was silky soft. He liked being with her despite her roundness. She had only one defect: she was very demanding when it came to sex. More than demanding, capricious. That would not be so bad were it not for her dimensions. Between her exigencies and body mass, he'd always wind up exhausted. Spent.

He could never possess her as she demanded. But barring that, Montse was an excellent person, a wonderful woman. Coming to this conclusion, Gerard Essomba didn't think that her plumpness was very important. It was just a blemish.

Roser was different. Very different! She was not as good a person, less generous. You could almost say she was a tightwad. She never gave him anything. But these problems wouldn't be so bad if it weren't for something else. Roser's biggest problem was her personal hygiene. From the moment he met her, Gerard Essomba had noticed her habits were filthy. He'd never known a woman who didn't wash herself before getting dressed. Every time he observed this in Roser he remembered his sisters when they were girls. After they got out of bed, if one of them did anything before washing herself, their mother would scold her. "The first thing a woman should do after getting up is go to the bathroom and wash their intimate parts, their face, and their teeth." That behavior was part of a ritual. And when he saw Montse comply with this command, he thought she must have been well parented. But Roser was different. The only thing she took care of was her face. After getting dressed she spent lots of time in front of the mirror putting on make-up. Often when he saw her do this he had the urge to ask her why she didn't wash her face before she painted it. But he said nothing for fear of losing his job. He had no recourse but to put up with her bad-smelling mouth, her underarms, and the disagreeable feel of her dry, coarse skin.

He regretted that Montse had not offered to marry him. He was sure he would not have hesitated to say yes. She wasn't exactly a woman he could take to his village as a trophy, but she could pass.

He imagined his arrival to his town with his new wife. People would come out of their homes to see them in their luxury car. But when they saw the woman who accompanied him, they would find it strange. The fact that she was white might impress them, so he'd have to deal with the envy of his childhood friends. And his parents would be proud when they caught a glimpse of him with his big, shiny car. His father would be even more proud wearing the suit, tie, and hat his son would have sent him from Europe. His mother would be wearing a beautiful new dress. "My wife pick it just for you," he would say.

But then again, what about the young women in his town? When he remembered them, his enthusiasm wilted. The girls in his town tended to be very cruel to men who married outside the village, no matter the color of their skin or where they were from. They would examine his new wife from head to toe and they wouldn't forgive a single defect. Surely when they first saw Montse, they would not hesitate to make a sarcastic remark like, "Wow, Gerard Essomba, you left us to bring back a white elephant?" And if that weren't bad enough, if just one little kid heard that stupid comment, he would lead a chorus when he and his wife went out for a walk: "Gerard Essomba—he brought us a white elephant!"

Those little shits! thought Gerard Essomba. *They're all a bunch of savages who don't know a classy lady when they see one!* The possibility of becoming an object of ridicule to the children of his town discouraged him. Fortunately Montse had not asked him to marry her. But if she had, he would not have turned her down just because of those beasts' foolish insinuations. No matter. He would have married her, and he would have introduced her to his people.

But what about Roser, what would they say about her? Surely nothing. Roser was thin, elegant, and daunting with a cigarette in her mouth. They would never know she didn't wash her mouth or her private parts. And of course he would not let them know, of course not!

After reflecting on the facts, Gerard Essomba was relieved. He wouldn't have a problem with Roser when they went on vacation. But Montse was the one he loved. That made him sad, and even sadder when he remembered all that had happened to him when he left his country: traveling across the desert, his stay in Melilla, his arrival to Barcelona. He asked himself how he might have not accepted Roser's proposal. But then again, God might punish him for his abandonment of the person who had taken him out of homelessness.

God had helped him a great deal. The Lord had always shown that he loved him. How many friends had failed in their pursuit of what he had obtained already? Many had died along the way. Others were homeless in other European cities. Others couldn't take it in their new environment, and they fell into drugs or petty crime and kept landing in jail. All things considered, he was the privileged one.

He thought about what his life would be like if he declined Roser's proposal. If Montse had him just for herself maybe their relationship would become too precarious, and they would have to cut it off. Then what? He could work, but at what kind of job? He knew what work was like for immigrants like him in Spain. He saw what they did. They only got the jobs that white people would not take. And they worked hours and hours for miserable salaries, leading only to hunger. When he came across these people, he would always hear the same thing: "My brother, life in the land of the whites is hard."

But he no longer had to endure that kind of life, the life of his African brothers. It was true that he was not sleeping well on account of his work, but at the same time he had the entire day to sleep. He ate well, and he even become knowledgeable about wines, even though he abhorred them at first. When he went to an African restaurant in his neighborhood and they offered him a cheap wine, he asked if there wasn't anything better. He liked to pretend he knew more by asking for a fine wine whose name he had heard. They never had it, of course. So, with a disdainfully arrogant tone, he said, "Okay, just give me a beer."

Gerard Essomba thought maybe he'd come too far, too high to fall, and if he had to return to that old life he wouldn't be able to endure it. God had helped him climb. Roser wasn't the woman he would have liked to marry, but what if it was God's plan? He had to know how to read the signs. God always uses signs to guide human beings.

All this made him think of a story he heard in his hometown. They said it came from the Jews. He didn't know, and since everything in the Bible comes from the Jews, they were probably right. He had never read this story in the Bible, but it very well could've come from the Sacred Scriptures. The story was about a priest. A torrential downpour had flooded the area where the priest was carrying out his mission. The priest climbed to the top of the church because the town was being evacuated. A boat arrived with many people, and the people asked the priest to come with them. The priest declined, saying that God would find a way to save him. A second boat passed, and like the first one, the people on it asked the priest to come with them. Again the priest said no, that God's great work on this land indicated that He would not abandon him. The ones who arrived on the third boat told him this was his final opportunity. But the good priest insisted on waiting for God's salvation. He said once again that God would indicate his road to salvation.

As one would expect, the waters reached the top of the church, and the priest drowned. He arrived at the gates of heaven perplexed. He asked to see God so that he could ask Him why he had put an end to his life so soon. God's secretary gave him an appointment with God, specifying the day and the hour. He waited, and when it was time, he gave the secretary his name and asked him why God had given him so little time. The secretary pondered the question and said, "Well, what I see here is that you were in a tight spot, and when God found out about it, he sent you a boat. But you turned it down. Then he sent you another boat, and you turned that one down too. And when you declined the third one, God interpreted it as a sign that you were tired of being on earth and that you wanted to die, and that's why He called you—to comply with your wishes."

Gerard Essomba concluded that after all his woes, Roser's proposal was like the third and last boat sent to the priest. If he relied on Montse to save him, it would be a mistake, like turning down all the boats as the priest had done. To say no to Roser would amount to wishing for his own perdition. When he arrived at this conclusion, he was terrified. He began to tremble. He ran to his cell phone. When he found it, still shivering, he entered Roser's number.

"Roser," he cried as soon as he heard her voice on the other side of the line. "I go with you!" Stunned by his quick decision, she was silent for a moment. Her silence worried him, so he asked if she had heard him.

"Yes, I hear you, but don't you think it's a little early? Have you thought about it?"

Roser herself now doubted the entire new arrangement. She hadn't known if the African would accept, and his call just a couple of hours after he had left her apartment took her by surprise. She also wanted to rid herself of the tremendous burden of guilt for wanting to take the man away from Montse. She had to make it clear that she wasn't the one taking him away, that it was he who had offered to accompany her.

Without realizing it, that short silence caused intense consternation on the part of the African. He suspected that perhaps the two women had tried to trick him into choosing between them. *God, what if that's true?* But when he heard Roser's answer he was relieved. Yes, he said. He had thought about it and his mind was made up. He told her this in a slightly docile tone. Still, he was not as certain as he had been before calling Roser. Up to that point he hadn't imagined that it could all be a charade. Now he had his doubts. So he kept up his defenses. If it were a trick, he would tell them that he'd known about it, but that he had pretended to go along just to see how things would turn out.

"Good, Gerard Essomba, go ahead and start packing. And like I told you, don't tell anyone, not even your friends. Tell them you're going on a trip and that you'll be back in a few days."

These directions reassured him. Yet his doubts persisted. It was still possible that the two natives were playing a cruel joke at his expense. The rest of his day was filled with anguish. He prayed to God several times, imploring Him not to abandon him. In the afternoon he did something he'd never done before. He went out to buy groceries, lots of them. He prepared a dinner, and when his two roommates arrived he invited them to eat with him.

The others were expecting the invitation. Gerard Essomba had bought a bottle of wine. Before pouring a glass for his friends, he spilled a few drops on the floor, as he murmured something of a prayer. It was directed to his ancestors: "I know I have abandoned you," he said. "But today I'm returning to you because I need help." Then he went back to the table and served the wine to his friends.

Gerard Essomba, like the majority of his fellow Africans, no longer believed he was living in communion with his dead ancestors.

Not long after he arrived at the city, he had embraced the faith of the Pentacostal Church of the Truth of Jesus Christ Sole Savior. It was one sect from among the thousands or perhaps millions that flood Africa these days. But he had suddenly, without knowing why, felt the necessity of relying on his ancestors for their wisdom, in a ritual he'd seen his grandfather perform. His father had recommended it after his grandfather's death: "When things are going badly for you and you are alone, don't forget the spirits are close to you. Call them," said the man responsible for his birth. He'd felt that loneliness in the face of hardship before, but at those times he had invoked God. But now he remembered his father's advice. And at that moment he pondered many of the same things that trouble so many Black Africans. They try to ascend to heaven to be with God with the same speed they descend into the bowels of the earth to find their ancestors. This lack of certainty or permanence, in either heaven or earth, has turned them into mental wanderers. This provoked an African thinker to proclaim that, in order to find balance, Black Africans should make sure they pay God for a trip to heaven. But Gerard Essomba was oblivious to this.

After performing that little ritual, he was somewhat relieved. While he would have preferred to be much more certain than he was, he did feel more confident. He spent Friday night at his place as Roser had advised, and on Saturday he kept his appointment with Roser at her apartment.

When he saw she was packing, his anxiety diminished. She hadn't taken many things out of the living room so as not to create the impression that she was leaving, but it was clear from the bedrooms that she was preparing for a long trip. The two of them pretended they weren't nervous, but they were. Suspicion had overcome their minds: Gerard Essomba of Roser, and Roser of Gerard Essomba.

The African wanted to reassure himself that this woman was not deceiving him. She often paused while she was packing. Indeed the packing could very well be part of the trick. It was still possible that Roser was just testing his loyalty. Or maybe both of them were in on the game.

Roser in turn was unsure of the African's determination. She feared he might betray her and declare he was exclusively in love with Montse. And if her friend discovered the deception, not only would she hate her, but she might also make the African a counter-offer. She knew Montse would not ask him to marry her, because she had no intention of abandoning her social surroundings. But she could offer him something very lucrative, and that possibility worried Roser.

The next day, Sunday, when Gerard Essomba was to be at Montse's place, both of them were filled with even more anxiety. "Above all, don't be nervous," Roser told him. "Just act normal. Don't let her notice anything."

Gerard Essomba told her she needn't worry.

At the indicated hour, he was waiting. He tried to distract his mind, but he couldn't. He was unsure of what to do. His head wanted to think that everything was going as planned, that this was not a game conjured up by the natives. But he still doubted. He kept asking himself if Roser's actions were just part of the game. Who can trust the whites? Sometimes they're strange. He'd seen some TV programs where the characters were always playing tricks on each other. But the victim never figured it out until the end. Considering these women had put their sexual fantasies into motion, they could very well have devised a macabre game at the Black man's expense—just to test him or to laugh at him. Gerard Essomba prepared himself for the worst.

And if it wasn't a trick—part of his heart assured him it was not—he admitted to himself that his behavior left much to be desired. He had no idea how all of this had come to be. But he did know that Montse was the person who had come looking for him. She had always been friendly to him. She had come to him that day in the hospital when his friend died. She had understood when he revealed that his former name was false. And most important of all, she had devised a work contract so that he could get his papers legally.

That was the person he was about to betray. Of course he didn't want to do it, but if he turned Roser down, what would become of his life? As he asked himself this question again and again, he saw Montse's car arrive.

"How are you, Gerard Essomba?" she asked with her usual affability.

"Fine, fine." But his voice trembled.

"How weird! You didn't say, 'Oh, yes,' like you usually say." She imitated his voice.

He forced a smile as he asked her if he had not used his usual expression.

"No, you did not say, 'Oh, yes.' I thought it was strange because you always say that."

He shrugged his shoulders.

"Would you like to go somewhere before we go to my place? I love spring evenings."

"Oh, yes." This time he sounded like himself and added that he'd like to go for a drive. Actually, he was pleased by the offer because the last thing he wanted was to be alone with Montse in her house.

"Well, that's what I like to hear. And where would Mr. Essomba like to go?"

"I... The place you take me in mountain first time? View of the city?"

"Well that's where we'll go. But I'll let you know that you've omitted your favorite expression again."

He didn't answer. He was boiling inside. He stared out the car window. Most of all, he didn't want to think. He knew that if he allowed himself to reflect, he would be drawn back to the Bible. He would see the finger of God pointing at him as if he were a bad person. He would end up comparing himself to the Sacred Scripture's worst pariah: Judas himself.

The streets were nearly deserted that late Sunday evening, despite the nice weather. They started up the hill in the neighborhood of Vallvidrera. When they got to the same spot they had first visited, Montse parked the car. "We have arrived. Mr. Essomba has been served," Montse said as she applied the hand break.

They got out of the car and looked up at the clear night sky. The small moon looked far away with only a few stars near it.

"Look how beautiful the sky is! Is there a pretty sky in Cameroon?"

"Oh, yes," he said. He spoke of the beauty of the Cameroonian night sky. He made an attempt to use his usual expressions so as not to call attention to his nervousness. But when he talked about his native Cameroon, he filled with longing. He spoke of it almost wishing that the remembrance of his country would relieve him from the anxiety that was consuming him.

"When you were little, what would you do on a night like this?"

"Oh, yes. We play at night, moon is our light. Dance, tell stories, very pretty. I listen to grandfather's stories. Many good stories."

He looked down at all the lights in Barcelona. The vista encompassed Barcelona in all its infinity, and that infinity took him back to the town of his childhood. He wanted to be a child again, to dream he was back there again with the other children. And like those other children, he also dreamed of being a doctor, or an important person like a government official—like the vice-governor of his province. Lord, would someone please take him back to those days! He also thought he could never imagine betraying the only person on earth besides his mother and father who had treated him with such understanding and tenderness.

"I'd like to go to Cameroon one day and gaze into the night sky on an evening like this one, to watch the children play and tell stories." Montse spoke with remarkable simplicity and sincerity. Because when people know each other intimately, their relationship becomes more fluid. Mutual understanding improves, mistrust and separation diminish. Montse's words brought Gerard Essomba back to the present. He felt tremendous remorse. His suspicion that Roser was playing a cruel joke had dissipated. The betrayal that most concerned him now was his own—his betrayal of the one who had helped him most. Cameroon, he told her with sadness, was not in good shape now.

"Much poverty in all of Black Africa," he said.

"I know, but one day things will get better. Other parts of the world have gone through similar hardships. Years, maybe centuries, but things improved. In Europe we're doing well, but we too went through a lot: cruel and absurd wars. I don't doubt that Africa will have its day. Places always do—"

He did not let her finish. He insisted that better days were not on the horizon.

"Sure, it will be difficult, but the good times will arrive eventually," she insisted. "But in any case, all I want to do is watch the children play and tell tales."

Her optimism was not convincing. "Government bring pretty roads and lights," he said, but then he added that that was the work of the Germans. Besides, he pointed out, the children no longer played or told stories. She could not believe that. "Oh, yes, now watch TV in house, and men drink in bars."

"What a pity!"

Gerard Essomba turned his eyes again to the lights of Barcelona. There it was. From that point, he could see almost everything. Beautiful. Luminous. The way only Barcelona can be at night. And even more so—as Montse reminded him—in the springtime. From Montjuic, it was as if they were on the rooftops of all the buildings, rooftops that conceal at once great truths and great lies: riches, and at the same time, much poverty; the big spirit in some, and the narrowness of others. He looked to his right. That night there were only two cars parked there, both with couples inside them. Gerard Essomba told Montse that fewer people felt the need to hide.

Montse laughed, leaned toward her friend's ear, and said, "It's that today is Sunday, and most people stay at home with their families. They can't find excuses to go out."

"Oh, yes. I see."

"Well, I'm glad you understand, because that's what we have to do too, go home and be like a family and do what everyone else does." She invited him to get back in the car. They got in and started down the hill. Once they were back at Montse's place they had dinner before getting into bed.

While they were having dinner Gerard Essomba tried to act as though nothing was happening. As Montse came and went from the dining room to the kitchen and back, he observed as many of the house's items as he could, so that he could remember them for the future. He forced himself to eat. He wasn't hungry, but he didn't want Montse to notice. It would have been strange for him—who always ate everything on his plate—to turn down a good steak like the one she had prepared. It was his favorite, along with fufu sauce.

"What did you and Roser do today?" he heard Montse ask him.

"In house. I watch TV."

"Did Roser go out?"

"Yes, short time."

His heart was beating fast. Lord, what torture! Is this what Judas went through before he betrayed Jesus? Judas knew he had sold him out but he acted like he'd done nothing wrong. Gerard Essomba was an avid reader of the Bible, so he knew he was behaving the same way as Judas. That is, if this whole plan wasn't a trick. He had seen members of his congregation throw themselves on the floor during services, desperately crying and beating their breasts. Never before had he understood why they flagellated themselves. He never thought much of them. But now he thought they should cry more, to express as much sorrow as possible. The more remorse the better. Because people are sinners, like him, and he was a sinner at that moment.

With his face in her hands she kissed him. He immediately moved his face to her chest. He needed it. He pressed his face into the woman's breasts and kept it there for awhile. Then mechanically, automatically, he drew back his head just a little and began to kiss his partner's nipples. He had no desire to make love, but he had to concentrate on his work in order to evade the lasting, tortuous shame he was feeling. He had to return to his task and carry out what he promised. He couldn't say no if he didn't want to arouse suspicion. This was his job, both women were his employers. So he gave it his best effort.

Since Roser had communicated her plan to leave the country with him, they had not made love. The lack of interest in sex, unusual for either one of them since he met them, was what convinced him that the plan was serious. He heard Montse moan with pleasure, sounds that brought him back to the reality of that moment. He went right to the task. He got on top of her.

"You're in a hurry, aren't you, my love? You must have missed your Montse."

Gerard Essomba entered her with difficulty. Suddenly he realized that he was not erect. It was as if his prick were dead. He tried touching it. Nothing. When he saw that she could tell he was soft, he told her embarrassingly that he didn't know what was wrong.

"Don't worry about it, precious, you're nervous. I could tell you couldn't wait to get inside me. Well, here I am, do it slowly like you usually do," she said affectionately.

Gerard Essomba did what he could to awaken his listless member, but it was out of commission. And the more he tried to make it rise, the less response he got. He resigned himself to his uselessness and opted for another method. He put his head between her legs and began to caress her clitoris with his tongue. Every now and then he checked on his dick to see if its status had changed, but nothing. Now he was worried. Visibly nervous. God! What was happening to him? Was he becoming impotent?

Oblivious to the mental torture her lover was experiencing, Montse kept on moaning and reached orgasm several times. But the African was still distraught. This had never happened to him. Was God punishing him? Was Montse unwittingly using her witch powers to take revenge for his vile deception? Gerard Essomba recalled childhood stories he heard in his village about the whites. Some described the whites' witchcraft and how they could figure out what people were thinking. Did Montse possess that kind of power?

The African touched his penis again. Still flaccid. He grabbed it and shook it vigorously. No response. Montse must have had powers: the magic that prefigures evil or ill intention. That was his conclusion. There was no doubt about it. He had lost. His prick was dead and it would not come back to life until he confessed his sin.

Montse, still unaware of the hell he was enduring, decided to change positions. She went for the one they both liked. She got on her knees. Gerard Essomba then stood up, making sure she couldn't see him or his wilted sex. It seemed to have fallen between his thighs like a branch from a dried out tree. He remembered the trees around his village that fell to the ground when he and his father cut them down to clear a space for corn or yucca, or malanga. He grabbed his member with two hands and moved it to the opening of the woman's vagina. It was a difficult task given her dimensions. He shook it again, as hard as possible. It was just not responding.

"What's wrong today, sweetness?"

He heard her. He knew he'd been discovered, but he didn't know what to tell her, only that something was wrong and that it was beyond his comprehension. He was on the verge of tears.

"Don't worry, my love. Just don't get nervous. It'll come back. Just keep on doing it to me like you do, you know I love it."

Ay, God, what a good woman she was! With a woman like that, how could anyone or anything ever hurt him? He obeyed. He lowered his head down to her legs, beneath her ass. Once there he assumed the position of a mechanic looking under the body of a car. He then did as she asked, only that it was impossible for him not to be nervous. He was both anxious and, above all, worried. It was possible he might be impotent forever. His entire life! Magic and witchcraft does that kind of thing. Men can be turned into eunuchs. Or they could wind up dead. And if he did not die, he was sure that his dick was finished.

Montse kept right on moaning, his tongue all over her as his mind jumped from thought to thought, going a mile a minute to a thousand different places, coming and going. Some thoughts calmed him. Others tortured him: questions, replies, negotiations, affirmations. Was he the one God had punished? Was the Lord the one who was making him suffer for betraying the person who had been so good to him? It couldn't be! It was God who had given him that opportunity. He was convinced his sudden impotence was a result of white people's magic. Whites had mind-reading powers that allowed them to get revenge for a dastardly deed, no doubt about it. So should he confess what he had done to Montse? Maybe his penis would come back to life. But at the same time he swore he would not tell her anything. He had sworn on his father's name, and, worse still, in the name of God. And the Bible forbade taking the Lord's name in vain.

Was it Roser's magic that was killing his manliness? Was Roser warning him with her witchery that he better not say anything?

Montse was enjoying herself as she felt her lover's tongue, from one orgasm to the next. She had become skilled at feeling her way there. She was absolutely unconscious of the African's terrible predicament as he continued working his mouth and tongue into her. But as he kept checking the status of his member with his hand, he became more convinced that the white magic was keeping it dormant.

"My God, have pity on me!" he cried desperately in his native Bulu.

Montse heard him. She stopped moaning for a moment to listen. She lowered her head to try to make out her lover's expression.

"Did you say something, my love...?"

Gerard Essomba realized he'd made a mistake. So he sucked his woman's genitals more fiercely. She reasoned that he had just let out a sigh of pleasure, and this excited her even more. And in a moment of profound ecstasy she let herself fall on top of him. Gerard Essomba, with his face covered in Montse's secretions—the sweat of her inner thighs, and perhaps even his own tears—

struggled to keep from suffocating. Once again, when he finally got out from under her, he breathed in deeply.

Then she turned around. "Come here, my little one," she said, as she extended her arm to him. He moved back over to her side. "You're acting a bit odd tonight. Anything wrong?"

Gerard Essomba was at the verge of confessing everything to her. If Montse had not been so big and had her enormous tits not kept her from feeling the rapidity of his heartbeat, she would have known he was distraught. Again he told her nothing was happening, just that he was tired. He didn't even think he could talk. His own words sounded like they weren't his. Because all he wanted was to tell the truth, to get back to normal, especially in regards to his manhood. Roser had tremendous influence over him. She was perhaps even the cause of his impotence. But if he told Montse the truth, it would perpetuate the state of his deadly tired member, maybe for life. These possibilities agonized him.

"Of course you're tired. We haven't been together in a long time. It's Roser's fault, the little slut, she has used you up," Montse joked. "But don't give it a thought. I'm sure you'll be ready tomorrow, like new. That Roser is going to get an earful! You better believe it! I'll tell her to think about someone besides herself."

She caressed his face. Then she slid her hand down his body to his cock. She touched it tenderly. "You'll see. Tomorrow you'll feel better, my little sweetness."

Minutes later she was asleep. Gerard Essomba tried to sleep too, but he couldn't. He was a mess. In addition to his anguish over the plan to leave with Roser, now he had to deal with the death of his prick. Death: that's the word they used in his town when a man's penis quits working. And what if it was really, *really* dead? He asked himself this over and over again. He kept on touching it. For an instant he thought it was rising, but then it fell, again…

Roser couldn't sleep. At one in the morning she was having her zillionth coffee. She wasn't sure if the African would keep his word. God, she didn't know a lot about Black people. She had read a book that explained why Blacks are like children. That was a long time ago. Had they changed? Unfortunately she hadn't had the time to observe Bambara Keita—or Gerard Essomba—closely. Why hadn't she? Now she knew him a bit better. At the beginning she had treated him with indifference. He was just a sex object, something like a vibrator. That's why she didn't pay attention to his demeanor or his actions. She cared more about how he interacted with the neighbors than anything else. It had been too late when she came to the conclusion that she was madly in love with him. She didn't know how to interpret her own feelings until her boss told her she had to move to Berlin. It was then that she realized how lost she'd be without him. Who would have thought that she, Roser Calatabuig Pons, would have fallen for a Black guy?

Lord, why didn't I take notice of him before? She had read in a novel by a woman from the US that Blacks are very proud. Maybe that was also true of all Africans. Yes, that was probably true. Africans were just like that. Her Gerard Essomba was man enough to keep his word. And if he decided not to go with her, at least he'd never say anything to Montse. His lips would be sealed.

But what if that wasn't true? What if Montse saw he was nervous and started firing questions at him? Would he keep the truth to himself? And if he gave in, what would her friend's reaction be? Surely she would rush over to her place and accuse her of God knows what.

Roser, too, was filled with anguish. She listened intently to the passing footsteps to see if anyone stopped in front of her door. She expected the doorbell to sound any minute. She listened for the telephone, anticipating a ring. It could be that Montse had decided not to come and see her but to call instead. She stood up and paced the floor. No night had ever been as long as this one. When it was four in the morning, she couldn't take it any longer. She decided to carry down her things and put them in the car that the company had provided to take her to the airport. She had left her own car in the building's parking lot.

When all her things were in the car, she went back up to make sure she hadn't forgotten anything. Everything was in order. Not much luggage; she had only taken the objects of greatest necessity. When she got to Germany, she would tell her parents where she was.

She started the car and left her apartment behind. She decided to drive around until it came time to pick her African up at the Plaza de Cataluña. If she didn't see him, she would know he changed his mind. She didn't want to dwell on that possibility, it was too painful. She kept her cell phone on, deciding she would only answer if she saw Gerard Essomba's number. She drove around without a definite destination. She thought perhaps she would watch the sun rise from the beach near the port. But she decided against that since Montse's office was close by. Although she thought about going toward her old office, she didn't dare go in that direction. Should she drive outside of town? No, not a good idea. The traffic would start to get heavy soon. Better to just drive around.

In the morning, Montse and the African got up early, as usual. Montse took him back to his usual place.

"You're very sad. Don't worry, everything will be all right. Go home and rest. I'll call you, and I'll come pick you up as always. If I get tied up, I'll let you know."

When he was on the street, he shut the door. She drove off. He didn't move until she disappeared from his view. He had a strong urge to cry. And he did. The Plaza de Cataluña was deserted at that hour. He sat down on a bench to rest a bit. Then, with his eyes still red from crying, he went to his dwelling.

His suitcase was packed. He got dressed and by ten he was waiting for Roser at the same plaza he had been in just a few hours ago with a big suitcase and a handbag. It was the place that had been his home for several months—cold in the winter and hot during the summer. It was a lonely home that filled up with people in the daytime, the where a stranger had made friends with him, saving him from that loneliness. As he waited, he kept gazing at the Plaza de Cataluña. He didn't know if he would ever see it again.

He heard a car horn. He was waiting at the bus stop to the airport. It was Roser. She stopped, and without getting out of the car she opened the door for him so that he could put his things inside. He got in and they drove off.

Along the way, Roser stopped the car. "Excuse me, I'll be back in a minute." She got out and walked to a post office, but he didn't know where she was going, and he was too sad to find out. They had barely spoken during the entire ride. They both felt like two outlaws, guilty of a terrible act of betrayal.

Gerard looked at himself. He was elegantly dressed. He was wearing a smart gray suit with a blue shirt—an expensive shirt, a well-known brand. But it was none other than the one Montse had bought for him. The silk tie as well: a gift from Montse. The watch too. Gerard Essomba shook his head in dejection.

Roser got back in the car and started it. "I just sent Montse a letter. I've explained everything that's happened, and I've asked her not to resent us. I'm sure she'll understand."

The African wasn't listening. All he said was, "Fine."

When they got to the airport parking lot, Gerard Essomba took the suitcases out of the car and went looking for a cart. Roser had told him that as soon as they arrived at the airport they should both act as though they weren't traveling together. They might run into someone she knew, maybe even on the same flight. Roser locked the car, put the car key in an envelope, and walked off with the African following, pretending to be on his own. Once she was in the airport, she signaled for him to wait for her. She left the key in a designated mailbox.

They went immediately to international departures. Roser had bought him a first-class ticket; hers was purchased by the company. She kept an eye on him. They wouldn't feel comfortable if they were sitting next to each other, but she wanted to be sure he was close by.

After checking their luggage, Roser discreetly signaled him to follow her. They went toward security. She stayed in front of him, and he followed, always docile. When they got to the waiting area for their gate, Roser sat down. Gerard Essomba did the same, two seats over from her. They had an hour before boarding. There was hardly anyone waiting.

Gerard Essomba looked around. He had never seen such a luxurious airport. When he arrived in Barcelona, the National Police put him on a hermetically sealed mini-bus. None of the passengers in that mini-bus had seen the airport. They took them directly to cells at the detention centers controlled by the police. And now that he had the opportunity to travel like an elegant gentleman, a free man, he was still unable to travel unsupervised. He was on his way to Germany, of all places! Germany, the European country most admired by his compatriots, because it was one of the first colonial powers to colonize his country. Indeed he should be happy. He should be proud of having achieved more than he had dreamed. But he wasn't happy or proud at that moment. He was traveling like a criminal, a fugitive. Happiness cannot be absolute. Life was not fair, but now was not the time to think about that. It would be a sin, and he didn't want to sin because he was a believer. Everything that was happening now was the work of God—that conclusion relieved his anguish.

Roser looked at him. She noticed his serious face. She was sad. *I'm sure he knows it as much as I do, we are doing a bad thing.*

She immediately suspected something. Was the African feeling remorse for what they had done together? Or was his sadness due to his feelings for Montse? She was jealous.

At that very moment, Gerard Essomba's cell phone rang. They looked at each other. "Don't answer it!" Roser ordered Gerard. She was almost shouting. The African took out his phone and saw it was Montse. He turned it off and put it back in his pocket. That action was a tremendous relief to Roser. She looked around to see if any of the other passengers had noticed them. No one had! They were reading their newspapers. She realized she should have told Gerard Essomba to turn off his phone when he got into the car.

Time moved slowly, until at last their flight was announced. Roser stood up and the African did the same. Always behind her, he got in line. Once they were on the plane, a flight attendant showed them their seats. Her seat was at the window on the left, and his on the aisle on the other side of the row. When all the passengers were seated, the plane began to move slowly away from the gate. They were on their way. Minutes later, as the plane ascended, they looked at each other as if they were partners in crime.

CHAPTER 13

IT WAS NINE AT NIGHT when Montse began to tidy up her office to go home. It had been an exhausting day—three meetings, one after the other. She called Gerard Essomba. She wanted to tell him she was on her way. But an anonymous voice answered. "The number you have dialed is not available at this time."

"How strange," she said.

She had called him that afternoon as she was on her way to one of her meetings, and she'd assumed he had turned off his phone. She didn't think much of it. She wanted to reassure him about his sexual competence, so she decided to call later. She had thought something was wrong with him the night before; he looked sad. Surely there was a problem. Maybe he got bad news from his family. She didn't want to pester him with questions. Everyone has a right to keep secrets in their own private life. All that could have an effect on his libido. She was sure that because of his young age he wasn't aware those things happen every now and then. She'd heard her friends talk about those kinds of malfunctions. It was annoying, they said, and she knew it was true because she herself had experienced it. But that's life. We aren't machines. And even machines can break down.

During the day she had not had a single moment free to call him. She entered his number the next day, and she got the same answer.

"Poor guy. I'm sure he's lost his phone, or maybe someone stole it."

She got out of her car and went to the place where she usually met Gerard Essomba. She didn't see him. She drove around the area, only to return to look for him again. No sign of the African. Montse was worried.

The department stores were still open. On the sidewalks in front of the big store entrances, street vendors of all races and origins—Asians, Africans, Latin Americans, Eastern Europeans, and people from other places—were selling their merchandise illegally. They sold ties, necklaces, pirated CDs and DVDs, shirts, and all kinds of other products.

Montse decided to park in the underground garage. As she walked up the stairs to the plaza, she looked for Gerard Essomba in the corner where she usually met him. But he wasn't there. To pass the time, she contemplated the street market, part of the economy that competed with huge department stores in defiance of the authorities. The illegal merchants had organized their stalls in two rows with spaces between each one. Montse walked along one of the rows to the end, then turned to go down another one. She barely looked at the merchandise. Occasionally, she looked toward the place where she usually met Gerard Essomba, but nothing. Her worries were becoming more and more intense. He hadn't been late since she met him. He was always punctual, always polite. She looked at her phone to see if he had called. Among the many calls that day, there was nothing from Gerard Essomba. She called Roser's landline. She heard Roser's voice saying she was not available and to leave a message.

Montse was tired of looking at the street vendors' items. She crossed the street. There were still lots of people at the Plaza de Cataluña. She turned around. She looked at the bench where she first met the man who used to call himself Bambara Keita. She smiled. If only she knew where he lived. She knew he shared a place with friends in the old part of town. That's what he had told her. But she never even asked the name of the street, convinced she would never have to visit that rough part of the city. But at that moment she regretted it. Her obsession with maintaining the privacy of their relationship deprived her even of the curiosity of knowing where he lived, the name of a friend, or a number where he could be reached in the case of an emergency. Something could have happened to him. Why didn't he call? And if he couldn't call, who could do it for him? The two natives had prohibited him from talking about their relationship with anyone, including his friends and roommates. The secret belonged to the three of them exclusively.

She looked at his number again: no calls. She called Roser again, both her cell phone and landline: no answer. She thought perhaps Roser had gone to the movies with the African, which would explain why their phones were off, but she couldn't imagine her going to a movie theater in Barcelona with a Black man. That made her smile. Could be. Who knows? People change, she thought. She really hoped it were true, even though she wasn't convinced of the possibility. Still, she was somewhat relieved. If Roser's and the African's phones were off, that meant they were together. She went back to the garage to get her car. Not to worry, she would learn of their whereabouts eventually. From her building parking lot she got in the elevator and exited on the ground floor to check her mail. As the elevator moved up to her floor she looked through the envelopes. Most were from the bank. But one was sent by express mail. Inside that envelope there was another one with Roser's name as the sender: Roser Calatabuig Pons. She opened the envelope just as she reached her floor.

She got out of the elevator, went into her apartment and shut the door behind her. She turned on the lights and placed her keys in her purse, the other mail on a table. She opened Roser's envelope. She had no idea what was going on. She found several pages handwritten by Roser:

Dear Montse:

When you read these lines, I will not be in Barcelona. I'll be in Germany...

"What the hell does this mean?" cried Montse. She sat down on the couch and turned on a reading light.

I know the damage I'll cause you when you find out what we have done.

"We?" Montse's heart began to beat fiercely.

Yes, I am using "we" because I have taken our man with me, Gerard Essomba.

"What? Where has she taken him?" Montse squeezed her eyes, bewildered.

A week ago, my company told me that they were moving me to Berlin to head a new office they just opened. At first I thought about telling you.

"It's not a joke!" Montse exclaimed, letting the letter fall to the floor. She grabbed the phone and called Roser. After hearing the greeting message followed by the beep, she said, "Listen, Roser, I know this is a joke. But I'm in no mood for jokes, so as soon as you hear this message call me, because I've had it with this!" She hung up. "This has to be a joke!"

She picked the letter up and continued reading:

I didn't tell you, Montse, because I knew you would not accept my proposal. This is very difficult for me. I'm not even sure how to begin. I found out abruptly that I was madly in love with Gerard Essomba, and that his absence would be very hard for me.

"What? Is she crazy?" she said to herself. "And what about me? Damn her! This can't be true!" She dropped the letter again and picked her phone back up.

"Margarita?" she asked when she heard Roser's mother's voice.

"Yes, it's me!"

"This is Montse. I wanted to know if you know where Roser is. She's not answering her phone."

"She's left for Germany. We didn't know. She just called us from Berlin to tell us that her company sent her there. I don't know why she's behaving this way, leaving just like that. I thought you knew about it. I was going to call to see if you knew anything..."

"I'm sorry, I didn't know," Montse said as she hung up, furious.

Montse cupped her face with her hands.

"I can't believe this! I just can't believe it! That bitch tricked me. She planned this trip without telling me so I wouldn't find out about her treachery! This is low! Really low!"

Montse shook her head. She grabbed the letter and continued reading. She desperately needed an explanation.

I don't know how this began, Montse. All I know is that when I found out they were sending me to Germany, a deep fear came over me just at the moment I was going to call to tell you all about it. I thought that when I left, I'd never see this guy again. At that moment, right at that moment, I discovered that I loved him with everything I've got. This probably sounds ridiculous to you, coming from me, but it's true. You're probably laughing. But maybe not, because you're probably so pissed off. Life is a surprise sometimes. Me, falling in love with a Black guy. I couldn't believe it, but that's the way it is, Montse. Suddenly I felt like a prisoner to my emotions, those silly feelings that both of us made fun of all the time.

I know it was you who started it. It was your plan, your design, your project. And I didn't cooperate. All I did was object. I could not have imagined that what started as a joke conjured up by a couple of sex-starved women would eventually turn into a source of conflict between us. A conflict because I know, Montse, that you'll never forgive me for what I've done. Believe me, it hurts me, and I'm so sorry...

"It's going to hurt *you*? You bitch!" she roared, pausing her reading. "What do you know about hurt? I did everything. And you put up obstacles every inch of the way. And now she's telling me she's sorry. I thought she was frigid and it turns out she's a snake in the grass!"

Montse's eyes began to fill with tears. She had been suppressing them, but this was too much. She let it out. She cried disconsolately.

"Why, Roser? Why? You were my best friend, like my sister. Joined at the hip! How could you have gone this low, how could you have screwed me like this?"

She went into the bathroom. She washed her face, and when she calmed down, she went back to the living room. She looked at the letter. She wanted to pick it up, but decided not to. She remained on the couch, staring at the wall. A deep bitterness began to eat away at her heart. In her mind she reconstructed the last few hours with Gerard as if it were a movie. Her man had been acting strange. Now she understood why. There had been a moment when they were all in her living room when she'd seen her friend looking at him with that sad look in her eye. He had averted her gaze. She didn't say anything to Roser then. Maybe Roser was suffering. Maybe she wanted to tell her something. What did that bitch offer Gerard Essomba to make him betray her like that? Something that she, Montse, had not given him? She had to know. Maybe the answer was in the letter. She continued reading:

I was terrified to be alone in Germany. I thought about the cold weather and the cold people. I know Germany very well, and I know the Germans. In my work I've dealt with them for a long time. They're all the same. I'm not as brave as you are, Montse, and I'm not telling you anything you don't already know. I never would have come up with the idea you planned for us. I know you can begin again. You can find another man like the one I'm taking away, but I could never do that. I don't have the courage.

"So you think I wasn't scared?" she cried. "You think it's so easy? You have no idea what I went through to find a good-looking Black man in the middle of the Plaza de Cataluña. In the heart of our, Catalonia!" Montse told herself that some people think everything is so easy. It was not so.

Roser's letter continued:

Suddenly I thought about my age. Without realizing it, as soon as you put your plan into action, you gave me energy. In spite of our little jokes, we pretended we had done away with our own sexuality, which is something that every human being so needs. But I realized it at once. And suddenly I saw myself old, traveling toward the end of my life, without any hope of finding a hand to accompany me.

"Cheap philosophy. You're full of shit!" She kept on reading. She needed to know if it said anything about the African.

It was not easy for me to come to this decision. I know that in spite of the rage you're feeling now because of the deception, you believe me.

"I don't believe a thing you're saying, not now or ever again, you damn whore!"

No, it was not easy. I'm ashamed of what I've done! These days have been tortuous for me. It's been hell. I never thought I could do such a thing. I knew sooner or later our plan would end. Because Montse, you know as well as I do, that eventually we would have had to tell the truth about Gerard Essomba. Suspicions would set in if they haven't already. A malicious neighbor or one of your family members might already suspect something about our double life. If you and I were truly free of the opinions of others, it wouldn't matter. But, my friend, we are prisoners of our society, even though we might think we're not. I don't think people like you and me will ever be free. If that were the case, we would not be doing everything we can to hide the man who has given us so much happiness. It's all about prejudices. This is the man who cured us of our ills and restored our faith in ourselves. Think about it, Montse, we aren't free. That's why we hide actions that are natural but cursed and prohibited by some people—or, better said—by our civilized society.

You never would have had the courage to confront your rich family if someone had come along and accused you of sleeping with a Black man in your house. Sure, some might say it's not true, that our society has changed, but you and I know that's not true. In fact, we have behaved according to society's norms. We showed affection to Gerard Essomba in the privacy of our homes, but when someone came around we immediately treated him with indifference. You did it and so did I. No, my friend, we are not free! Social prejudices that go as far back as The Crusades and conquests are very much alive today, all making it impossible for us to feel free. That's why I don't want to tell you that because I've taken him to Germany with me, I've liberated myself from those prejudices. I've still got them and I don't think I'll get rid of them for the rest of my life.

And I think it will be that way because I only realized that I love him when I was given the opportunity to go far away from the people I know. It's only because I'm going to live in a country where no one knows me. In Berlin I'll be able take walks with him without a care that I might be seen by someone I know.

I convinced him to come with me by proposing marriage. Yes, Montse, I'm going to marry him. In a way, you gave me that idea. You said that we in the West live in a paradise, according to the people of the Third World, and that in paradise you can do anything you want. I told him that after two or three years of our marriage he'll be eligible to become a Spanish citizen. What young immigrant would not accept my proposal? I've gone very low, haven't I? Possibly, my dear friend, perhaps what I've really done is bought my own life, my time, my happiness.

Although then again I shouldn't use that word "bought." It's more like I've borrowed it. Yes, that's it. I think I have borrowed my own life, my time, my contentment.

Two or three years next to the person I love means a lot to a person of my age. I know it's been difficult for him. I think that maybe if he could have chosen he would have gone for you, because I'm sure he appreciates you more than me, but I'm not sure he loves you. To convince him not to stay with you, I've had to tell him the truth. I've told him he'll never be able to be with you openly because your powerful family would never allow it. And you are very close to your family. So as you can see I've not only betrayed you, I've told him the truth about you as well.

No, I don't think he feels the same way about me! I know he would have preferred you. Have I ever told you he hardly ever kisses me on the mouth? I don't know why...

"I know why! It's because your mouth stinks!" Montse cried triumphantly. "He kisses me a lot, and passionately, you dirty little— He doesn't kiss your lips because your mouth smells like garbage! It was polite of me not to tell you, but you can bet I'm not going to my grave without telling you. Someday I'll tell you right to your face, you dirty whore!"

Montse was not swallowing any of the excuses Roser had written in her letter. None of what she said justified the betrayal. A friend is a friend. That relationship is sacred. But she wanted to hear every explanation that Roser came up with.

But I don't care. I suppose one day I'll ask, and he'll tell me.

"I'll tell you, pig: Your mouth smells like garbage! He'll be very reluctant to tell you the truth, but I'm sure he will eventually. Your mouth smells rotten. I should have told you a long time ago. I don't know why I didn't!" Despite her state of mind, Montse kept reading.

As I was saying, I know it has not been easy for him to decide to come with me. That's why I think he shares the blame. I gave him time to think about it, but only after telling him the truth about what he could expect with you. I imagine he too wants to live his own life, borrow a little life from his life and a little time from his time. We found him on the street, and my leaving meant to him that he would no longer be able to continue his life as it was, not alone with you. It's possible he did not see a way out. He had no choice. He is very young, and it's possible when he gets his citizenship from a country in the European Union, he might feel he wants to be completely free. I know this, and that's why I've offered to help him build a house in his native village. With that maybe I'll get a few more years. Four or five years at my age is almost like winning the game of life, my friend. But at the same time I'm not discarding the possibility that maybe one day he might love me, when he discovers my true feelings.

I've got two or three more years in Germany, so I'm thinking about asking for early retirement even if the company doesn't offer it before then. I'm not coming back to Barcelona, Montse. I've thought about it. I'll buy a house in the South, maybe by the sea in Almería, where I hope to spend the last part of my life, unless my husband decides to take me to his country. The last thing one can lose in this life is hope.

I know you will never forgive me, but still, I'm asking for it. I'm on my knees, my dear friend. My act is cowardly and vile, but I have had no choice: I've had to go through with it...

Montse tossed the pages of the letter to one side. She breathed deep. She was still angry. She was furious; she had done all the dirty work and all Roser did was take advantage of it.

Montse thought about what had happened. She considered her life's emptiness. She'd gotten all she wanted since the day she was born, but she had always felt there was something missing. Her physical appearance had not helped. She was not attractive to most men. Nor had she been able to take advantage of her family's money. It never seemed to trickle down to her. She had bad luck with men. She wasn't sure her failure in this regard was due to her weight. She just hadn't been fortunate that way. From the moment she'd initiated the adventure with the African months ago, she discovered a part of her life that had been missing. She discovered she liked sex. In a few months she was able to put her fantasies into motion, fantasies that were until then just that— pure imagination. Suddenly she found she was truly happy. She had her family, her work, her friends, but more than anything else, in the solitude of the night, she was able to enjoy the company of a man, a man she liked and who knew how to make love to a woman.

She no longer considered the African a sex object. He had become to her an indispensible companion. Sometimes she was uneasy about his being with her friend. But she enjoyed learning that they both felt that way. Thanks to that immense satisfaction, she realized her friend might be thinking the same thing. She had thought about the two of them, while Roser thought only of herself. How many times had she imagined herself walking down the streets of Barcelona with Gerard Essomba! At times she would say, *I wish he were just a little more white, so that my parents and my friends wouldn't object.* But when she thought about this, she also thought of her friend's feelings. She never thought in a million years that the only thing important to Roser was her own happiness.

This filled Montse with sadness. Roser had not returned her affection and loyalty. She was certain that at a certain time, she would have brought the African into her life openly. Her affection for him had been growing. She would have done anything for him.

She knew she would have found herself in a precarious situation if people had found out about her relationship with a poor Black man. But she also felt there was always a way out

It was three in the morning when she climbed into bed with difficulty. She felt defeated; her entire being had been destroyed. She couldn't sleep all night. Something was missing. She felt like part of her body was suddenly gone. Life is a matter of habits, and happiness depends on habit. She was now accustomed to having Gerard Essomba in bed at her side. She always waited for him with great anticipation and hope. That was happiness, those little moments after she left work, on her way to see the African, the man who talked to her about everything and nothing, and then they would make love. But now she was empty.

She didn't go to work the next day, alleging sickness. On Tuesday her family came to see her in the afternoon. She could not explain what was wrong. She'd always been a happy, extroverted person, but now she was sad, absent, pensive. She told them it was stress. She had been that way for a week, so she decided to seek professional help.

"Dr. Macarrulla?"

"Yes, it's me. Who is calling?"

"This is Montserrat Torres."

"Ah, yes, how are things with you?"

"I'm here, aren't I, doctor?"

"It's been a while since I've seen you."

"I've been away, doctor. I've been on a long trip alone."

"A trip, well then. Have you been back for long?"

"I just got back, and I need your services."

"Yes, of course. I'll talk to the receptionist and ask her to make an appointment."

"Yes, please, doctor. I need to see you soon, because in addition to the problems you know about, I have a new one, and I think it's worse."

"Really?"

"Yes, doctor. Aside from everything I had before, now I'm consumed with a desire to kill my best friend and a Black man!"

She didn't wait for his reply. She hung up. She breathed deeply. She was somewhat relieved to have blurted out her basest desire. She wasn't lying. She had an urge to kill her best friend, and while she was at it she'd kill the Black man, too—a Black man named Bambara Keita, or Gerard Essomba, or whatever. For the entire week, her hatred for them had not diminished. Just the opposite, it had gotten worse. And she did nothing to try to get rid of it. Her hatred knew no bounds. The last thing she wanted was to forgive the hurt they had caused her. And to top everything off, they had betrayed her in the springtime, her favorite and most special season. Every spring she felt renewed. She loved that time of year, and her friend and Gerard Essomba had chosen that season to destroy her. Her moment. Months she called her own.

Were Roser Calatabuig and Gerard Essomba really the only ones she would have wanted to shoot if she had a gun handy? Or was it that she wanted to execute whoever was responsible for all the evil, injustice, and ills of the world? For the moment, she could only think of those two.

TRANSLATOR'S AFTERWORD

INONGO-VI-MAKOMÈ'S *NATIVES* IS A NOVEL one might call "half serious." But which half? As the translator, I'd say the answer to that question is up to the reader.

English speakers and readers might need a little information before they decide which half of this novel is serious and which is humorous (or playful, or tongue-in-cheek, or ironic, or satirical). Does Inongo-vi-Makomè conceive of his main character Gerard Essomba (aka Bambara Keita) as a realistic representation of the hundreds of thousands of recent African arrivals to Europe, the ones we hear about in the media, who risk their lives crossing the Mediterranean or walking across the desert in hopes of escaping the misery of their native lands? That is, does this novel provide readers with an accurate picture of a sociological phenomenon? Just as importantly, is his portrayal of these two well-to-do Catalan women intended to represent the anxieties, wants, and frustrations of other European women of their ilk? Specifically, how are we to read the ending: is it a love tragedy? Is it meant as a social criticism of first world greed or indifference to the historical legacy of colonialism? Do these women, regardless of their obvious personal and physical differences, manifest more than just the silliness of the behavior of sexually frustrated women of a certain class? If the answers to these questions is yes, or more yes than no, then why are so many of the situations in the novel absurd, exaggerated, or just plain not believable? Or put another way, why is the African so stereotypically well-endowed? Given the descriptions of Bambara/Gerard's member, could the author make it as a stand-up comic playfully and painfully making fun of relationships between blacks and whites, especially the sexual ones, as he flaunts his own political incorrectness, thereby laying bare the unresolved tensions of those relationships?

Taking a stab at answering these questions, lets consider the life of this would-be stand-up comic, Inongo-vi-Makomè. He resembles Gerard Essomba, because he is from Cameroon. But the resemblance does not go much beyond that. Inongo, as he prefers to be called, was born in Cameroon, but unlike Gerard he learned Spanish at an early age. He is from Lobé, on the southeastern coast close to the border between Cameroon and Equatorial Guinea, which is a former Spanish colony. This provides at least a partial answer to another obvious question: why was this novel originally written in Spanish?

Inongo has lived in Barcelona for decades. He moved with his family to Equatorial Guinea as an adolescent and, unlike his main character, traveled to Spain not from a detention camp in Melilla like Bambara/Gerard, but as a student intent on finishing high school before going on to study medicine at the University of Valencia. His intention to become a doctor, however, was short-lived; he wanted to be a story teller. In a conversation[1] we had in 2009, he told me that he has always been a dreamer with an active imagination. And one of his favorite pastimes has always been to tell his son stories from his African, specifically Ndowe, tradition. Thus the preponderance in *Natives* of proverbs and tales conjured up by the main African character that so baffle and annoy Roser is at once a narrative ploy and a manifestation of the author's literary influences.

---

1. Interested readers can find the entire interview in the *Afro-Hispanic Review*, vol 30. no. 1, 2011, 165–68.

Moreover, the main character's political views, his criticism of the West's colonization of Africa, his questioning of the word "discover" in reference to Columbus's voyage to the Americas, his critique of the corruption of post-colonial African governments, his memories of his father and grandfather in the native land and their sanguine advice on life's trials and how to deal with them—all of this comes directly from Inongo's own world view and life experience.

Moreover it is important to take into consideration that Inongo is not alone as an African author who chooses to write in Spanish. In addition to the many Moroccan poets and narrators whose language of creation is that of Cide Hamete Benengeli's translator (or so the apocryphal narrator of *Don Quijote* tells us), there is an entire corpus of literature that comes from Equatorial Guinea and Western Sahara. It is among that group of contemporary Guinean writers and texts that Inongo's artistic production should be placed if we want to understand where he comes from existentially, politically, and geographically (a border area between a former French colony and a Spanish one). Indeed, Inongo shares the Equatorial Guinean exiles' sensibilities.

Also important is that Inongo is an accomplished writer. He has published three novels in addition to Natives, and three book length essays on the immigration-emigration of Africans to Spain. His novel for adolescent readers, *Akono y Belinga, el muchacho negro que se transformó en gorila blanco* [*Akono and Belinga: The Young African Who Turned into a White Gorilla*], addresses subject matter also worthy of adult attention. The book is something of a Cain and Abel story in which the murdered brother—Akono— dies only in the conventional sense. That is, in accordance with many African belief systems, he never actually dies, but instead travels to a different sphere, returning at times to the present world to screw things up. In this case the punishment for the killer—Belinga—is that he is turned into an albino gorilla. What follows illustrates the popular saying, "Be careful about what you wish for," because as a white entity he faces a complicated series of unexpected problems. All of Inongo's work contains anecdotes from the African tradition that not only tell a story but also teach his readers important lessons.

But Inongo's many publications have not received wide attention, for a variety of reasons. For that matter few if any of his fellow writers have received the recognition they deserve. Nevertheless Inongo, from his Barcelona residence, continues to write. "I can live off my writing," he told me, "but not in luxury," an understatement. At times he performs the stories and wisdom he has inherited from his oral tradition in elementary and secondary schools. He returns to the area of his birth at least once a year. At the moment he is struggling to collect funds to construct a youth center and library in his hometown. He is 67 years old, and I predict that he will continue to write and perform as he has done for most of his life, regardless of any unexpected recognition of his creative work on the part of Spanish or international literary society.

But back to *Natives*. This translator is still intent on allowing the reader to make her own judgment. But, perhaps as a cop-out, I'll say that I think it is precisely Inongo's intention to make his readers think about that fine line between comedy and seriousness. Monte's and Roser's relation with Bambara Keita starts out smoothly, at least in the practical sense. At first the only problem seems to be the size of the African's member—just too much for the skinnier Catalan woman to handle. But she not only gets used to it, she is thrilled by the ecstasy it provides. Of course, this African, like most African studs, is not only well endowed, he is handsome, clean, and respectful. Most importantly, he aims to please. This ménage à trois is a working relationship, and the narrator reminds us so on many occasions. Bambara Keita is a sex worker and he is the better for it, until things start falling apart. How could these things continue as they were? As the reader probably guessed not far into the novel, these two women will fall in love with the African sex-worker. They both end up wanting him for more than sex, and of course this desire leads to betrayal.

This is all very conventional, even predictable. But then again, that's the point. As the novel unfolds the three characters are cast into a series of circumstances where Catalan prosperity, home-less immigrants, Africans unable and unwilling to stay in Africa, Bambara/Gerard's story of how he ended up in Barcelona after spending over a year in a detention center in Melilla, and the *¿qué-dirán?* [what-will-they-say?] mentality of genteel Catalan society intersect. All this with regular interruption by an African oral tradition that compels the narrator to put the plot on hold so that his character can tell a story or two to anyone willing to listen. But as these stories come to us second- or third-hand, as in the oral tradition of the African griot, let's not react like Roser—incurious, clueless, presumptuous, insisting on the utter insignificance of these little stories. Since I'm a Hispanist, I am reminded of the many interpolated stories that reside in Spain's most acclaimed novel, *Don Quijote*. Frustrating? Perhaps, but readers who allow themselves the joy of reading, might—I hope—find them inter-esting in and of themselves, in the knowledge that eventually the narrator will take us back to where we left off.

I'd like the reader to know that this is the first time I've trans-lated an erotic novel, full of scenes that would make the nuns of Las Descalzas Reales Convent in Madrid cross themselves. *Dios mío*, say some of my friends, what a good time you must have had translating this. My response is no, no, no. I felt like what I imagine the cameraman experiences in the production of a pornographic video: the sex scenes are all about technique, simulating physical desire—poses, body parts, expressions, and fantasy, with just enough believability to make the whole thing work. In this endeavor, individual words are of utmost importance. That's why I chose, with my editor's encouragement, not to translate Inongo's oft-used word pene as "penis": it sounds too clinical, scientific, and insipid. Better "cock," "dick," "shaft," "rod," or other graphic, crude, or erotic word-images that simulate the illicitness of the three characters' activity.

There are many other translator's considerations I could mention, but one that stands out is the speech of the protagonist. How could I capture Inongo's realistic portrayal of Bambara/Gerard's dialogue, that of a man just having arrived, as it turns out, from French-speaking Cameroon? At times Inongo makes him sound ingenuous, unaware of his new environment, inarticulate. But at the same time, if we listen to what he says, he is anything but. Indeed Inongo's main ironic, tongue-in-cheek narrative/linguistic move is to debunk the stereotype of the "native," tribal Africans supposedly with no culture, language, technology, or sophistication, by turning the upper class Catalan women into the real "natives" of the title. That's the main joke, the humorous side of the novel. But once again we are left with the reality that Gerard Essomba describes on numerous occasions: he, like so many others, is in Europe to negotiate, to make a deal that will allow him to survive. That's why we readers need to listen to him—carefully, respectfully, openly, democratically, and thoughtfully. That's why I've translated this novel, and that's why I think—and hope—English-language readers will like it.

Michael Ugarte
Albacete, Spain
July, 2015

CPSIA information can be obtained at www.ICGtesting.com
Printed in the USA
LVOW10s0119260815

451441LV00005B/14/P